ONE-WAY TICKET TO APOCALYPSE

From the bow of the gunboat, Vic Gabriel stared down the river, peering into the darkness. The darkness was impenetrable. But when he looked inside, he found the darkness overwhelming, threatening to suffocate him with a burden he had never before known.

Like always, no matter how bad things got, Vic Gabriel would deal with the situation. There was never any other way. To run, to hide, to duck, to look for an easy alternative, is to die. Searching for the easy way had never been Vic Gabriel's way. The hard way is the best way, the only way, and if he was to die in Nicaragua, then he was determined to die like he had lived. The hard way.

Bantam Books by Dan Schmidt
Ask your bookseller for the books you have missed

EDGE
OF
THE BLADE

Dan Schmidt

BANTAM BOOKS

NEW YORK · TORONTO · LONDON · SYDNEY · AUCKLAND

EDGE OF THE BLADE

A Bantam Book / November 1990

ISBN 0-553-28807-5

Published simultaneously in the United States and Canada

Bantam Books are published by Bantam Books, a division of Bantam
Doubleday Dell Publishing Group, Inc. Its trademark, consisting of
the words "Bantam Books" and the portrayal of a rooster, is
Registered in U.S. Patent and Trademark Office and in other
countries. Marca Registrada. Bantam Books, 666 Fifth Avenue, New
York, New York 10103.

PRINTED IN THE UNITED STATES OF AMERICA

OPM   0 9 8 7 6 5 4 3 2 1

For Ralph L.,
a good friend who never let it get too lean.

Chapter 1

Fire roared, blossomed into huge mushroom clouds, rolling, boiling in a series of titanic explosions across a burning cobalt sky. Flaming sheets and things that resembled men descended in a saffron-and-crimson rain over the jungle canopy. A winged behemoth, engulfed in flames, plummeted from a sky on fire, spiraling from a blazing atmospheric ring around the immediate ozone layer that seemed torn apart by explosions of supernovalike dimensions.

It went on and on for what seemed like an eternity, then the short, black-bearded man with the shark's-teeth necklace ordered, "Enough! Cease fire!" He triggered his AK47 skyward, demanding their attention.

Wreckage hammered the earth and AK47-toting Sandinistas, burdened with RPG-7s or radio backpacks, scrambled away from the downthrusting cyclone of fire.

A flaming behemoth crashed into the jungle and the earth seemed to tremble with rage as shrieking flocks of birds scattered from the tree line.

There would be no more killing because he had killed enough of them for the day. It was enough that the invaders understood they had been lured into their deaths by one of their own, that they had been outsmarted by what they considered an inferior fighting force of Marxist trash.

Survivors could expect the worst. Survivors would discover imperial *yanqui* arrogance was no match for Sandinistas who had put their lives on the line for *la revolución* for years.

And Comandante Miguel Horchiba Bonano had just

1

shown them that no agent, no paramilitary operative from the CIA, would leave the steaming jungles of Nicaragua. Alive.

Like hooking and reeling in the freshwater sharks of Lake Nicaragua, which was a devout hobby of his, Bonano and his two-hundred-strong army of anti-Somoza, anti–United States rebels had guided the armada of CIA C130 Hercules gunships to the savanna with radio equipment captured just days ago from a squad of Contras. Three of those ten gunships, all of them loaded down with hardware destined to fall into Contra hands, had just been shot out of the sky, and anyone aboard those flying death machines had never even known what hit them. The burning hull of one gunship was a smoking pyre, testament to the savagely one-sided surface-to-air RPG-7 rocket attack, and was now wedged in the jungle canopy, flames crackling and spitting from the foliage, tongues of fire reaching out for Bonano. Fire raced across the tree line, and Bonano heard the terrible shrieking of several *kongos*—howler monkeys—as they were lapped up in the blaze, small charred bodies dropping to the smoking earth behind the comandante like coconuts.

As he surveyed the scene, he knew that this was only the beginning of some monstrous web of CIA treachery. Rumors of an invasion were in the wind and the comandante feared that their borders with Costa Rica and Honduras were now being padded with an American troop buildup. It was possible, he knew. Anything was possible in war-torn Nicaragua. The hated CIA was everywhere, and wherever they were, there was sure to be deceit and lies and bloody violence. But Bonano had his own plans to thwart the CIA, and he would use their own people to do it.

As he walked, sweating and smiling among his victorious rebels—who shouted, "*Viva la revolución! Viva la revolución! Viva Bonano! Viva Bonano!*"—he felt at one with but also detached from the death and destruction. He had seen many die needlessly since the revolution of 1979, and there was nothing even remotely grand, he thought, or even noble about a war that would see no end in sight as long as the American CIA kept supplying the enemy Contras. A war where his people were tugged about by the Americans and the Russians, and it didn't matter if they were Contra or Sandinista—Moscow wanted a springboard into Mexico, and Washington was trying to prevent that no matter what the cost to human life and property, Bonano thought. A war where men, women, or children had died in countless droves, dying because of lies inflicted upon them by the two self-serving insatiable giants of the world. And the CIA and their rogue lackeys especially did not care who died. As long as Cuba and Moscow kept their weapons and their people out of Central America. As long as Moscow was prevented from turning Nicaragua into another Cuba.

The stench of roasting flesh piercing his nostrils, harsh sunlight beating down on his neck, Bonano, his AK47 hugged snugly around his shoulder, listened to the shrill screams of the enemy. Men died slow and painful deaths by machete. Skin stripped off their bones and raw dripping chunks stuffed into their mouths. Trousers removed and genitals hacked off. *Guerrilleros* lined the enemy up against the gunships and firing squads mowed them down. Again, Bonano ordered the killing to cease. Again, unhappy and disapproving looks were thrown at him.

Curtains of thick black smoke wafted over the savanna, and dozens of dead men, CIA-sponsored mercenaries and military advisers, were strewn across the savanna. It was an awesome display, Bonano thought, of renewed anti-Somoza, anti-American might. The Russians and their Cuban advisers may have been right, Bonano thought. The Americans were upscaling the war in Nicaragua.

It might have been just as well for the counterrevolutionary forces of the anti-Somoza freedom fighters. The trap had netted quite an impressive haul for Bonano. His men removed large wooden crates from the gunships and loaded them on transport trucks and scores of horse-drawn carts or strapped them to mules. AK47 autofire rang out across the savanna, and any enemy numbers who survived the hatred of his rebels were kicked and beaten and slung into carts to be taken to the garrison and interrogated. They were cursed and spat on, but Bonano could appreciate and understand their hatred of anything American.

"Comandante! Look!"

Striding away from the flaming ruins of two gunships, Bonano spotted Ramon Alvano Treguerrez. Treguerrez was displaying one of the hundreds of M16 assault rifles with attached M203 grenade launchers taken from the crates. Many of the rebels fired wildly into the air with the seized M16s, whooping and laughing.

Treguerrez displayed a set of yellow-stained chipped teeth in a broad grin. "This is the *nonbelligerent* aid the *norteamericanos* bring to Nicaragua. Liars! They are like vipers that slither through the high grass and strike when you least expect them to. But there is more, Comandante, much more. Rocket launchers. Grenade launchers. Thousands and thousands of clips for the M16s. Perhaps it is as we feared? An invasion?"

Bonano was about to voice his own fears of the rumored invasion when the earth trembled beneath his feet and thunder pealed across the sky. The Sleeping Lion!

A heavy silence fell over the savanna, and all heads turned northward, expressions carved in terror. Even the roar of nearby flames was extinguished by the rolling thunder. Even the screams and pleas of tortured men ceased at a sound that seemed to split the sky asunder and ricochet off the green wall of jungle.

It happened once in a while, but the fear always tore through him like a bullet and Bonano hated the taste of that fear on his lips.

The squat, topless cone-shaped mountain rose above the jungle tree line to the north. A chalky mist hung over the jungle in that direction, a long roiling shroud. The sun split the mist in jagged fingers and cast a cloaking blaze over the jungle and the spiny ridge of black hills to the west. But there was no mistaking the steam that puffed steadily from the lake of molten lava inside the throat of the Sleeping Lion. For as long as anyone could remember, the volcano had been dormant, but lately it had been rumbling and spewing ash and clouds of fine black dust into the sky. Traditionally, the Indians would hurl babies into the crater when the volcanoes of Nicaragua threatened to erupt, hoping to appease the gods. It was superstitious nonsense to Bonano, but eventually he had come to accept the dark beliefs of the local Indians. Lately, Bonano had helped to shape tradition. He would give the Indians live enemy bodies, either Contra or CIA, and watch them feed the wrath of the Sleeping Lion with something other than babies or small children, which he found distasteful.

Treguerrez sought out Bonano with eyes wide with fear. "The Sleeping Lion, he wishes to wake up."

Bonano pushed his fear aside and looked at several of the *norteamericanos* with contempt. "*Sí*. Perhaps the Sleeping Lion, he needs to eat."

Nervous laughter broke from the throats of the *guerrilleros*.

A delayed explosion puked a hole in a gunship fuselage, hurtling debris across the savanna.

And the Sleeping Lion rumbled.

Shouts of *Viva la revolución*, Bonano noticed, no longer held as much enthusiasm as before.

Chapter 2

Major Ben Ellis was at the breaking point. After three days of no food, no water, and suffering almost constant torture and interrogation, he was just about to tell the Sandinista comandante anything he wanted to hear. Anything. Even if it was pure bullshit. Every man, no matter how tough, how brave, he knew, passes that point of pain where there is no return, only an overpowering desire for the pain to stop. He'd seen it before, although he had been on the other side. Guys, a soldier's soldier you wouldn't think you could break, no matter how much pain you inflicted on him, no matter how many threats you made about removing his family in the most heinous of ways, would end up bawling like a baby and blubbering on with everything you wanted to hear and then some like there was no tomorrow. Broken to the point where you couldn't get him to shut up.

The major feared he had reached that point. When he started talking, he wouldn't be able to stop himself and that would be the end of the ballgame. He had already given the comandante invaluable intelligence about the arms delivery to the Contras but they still believed he knew more. Even if he survived this hellhole somehow and made it out of the jungle, he knew the Company would show no mercy. He had compromised himself and the mission, code-named Operation Deliver Us From Evil. He almost laughed when he thought about that code name for the arms shipment. Where do the brains at Langley come up with that kind of shit anyway? Maybe they needed to put in some hard time down here in Nicaragua, he thought, and see just what a

6

man of compassion and understanding their big buddy, Anastasio Somoza and his sons had been to the average peasants, who made up the majority of the country's population.

But it wouldn't be the typical CIA flimflam artists, the guys who pulled the strings on a campaign without having to resort to violence, who would come after him. They would send some animals for him, guys who laughed at the sight of blood and who had even been known to drink it from a target's corpse.

And they would track him down to the far corners of the earth, if necessary, and exact vengeance. Worse, he had been paid a flat fee of fifty big ones, a huge wad of dead presidents that would never see life in his hands, just take up space in the Bank of Nassau. That was some serious money for Langley to be shelling out, but he suspected something very serious was mounting and in the works. What exactly, he wasn't sure, perhaps an invasion of Nicaragua. Either way, he feared he wasn't going to be around to see it. He was dead, he knew, and all he had to do was wait for the end to be delivered to him from somebody.

Stripped to the waist, Ellis was hung from the ceiling, his hands bound together by rope. They had jacked him up off the dirt floor of the 12x14 cell a few inches so that he was forced to stand on his toes. Blood, where the ropes had chewed into his flesh, trickled down bone-lean arms caked with filth. The strain of that position alone was knifing excruciating agony through his body, but they hadn't stopped there. Far from it.

Long bloody weals, festering with ooze, streaked his torso. Mosquitoes buzzed around Ellis and picked at the glistening furrows of flesh where a machete, its blade heated to a glowing edge in fire, had been drawn across his ribs, chest, and stomach. He could still hear his own screams in his head. He could still feel his balls shriveling up in his sac every time they put the edge of the blade to him. He could still smell the sickly-sweet stench of his own flesh as it sizzled and burned. He had never known such pain before, and he never wanted to know such pain again.

In the corner of the cell, a bed of red-hot coals still glowed and the machete in question was impaled there, waiting to fire skin at the whim of the comandante. Three black rats, as big as small dogs, skittered in the shadowy nooks and crevices at the base of the cracked stone wall. A small iron-barred window behind the emaciated hanging figure let a few fingers of sunlight filter in. Sweat poured down the major's chest, and he felt congealed blood loosening up and forming a small pit of slimy muck in the crotch of his olive drab khakis. He could hear the shrieking of howler monkeys and the cawing of wild birds beyond his cell. He would have given anything in the world right then to trade places with them.

Had he gone soft? Had he gotten too greedy for a large sum of quick cash? Had he been too bored and restless with the sedentary life of a college professor teaching military history to a bunch of kids who didn't know their elbows from their buttholes, who didn't even know who Somoza was or who could not have cared less about communist encroachment on the Mexican border of the United States? What the hell was he even doing down there again? Money? Adventure? He wasn't even really sure he believed in the Contra cause anymore, because he had seen those CIA-backed rebels in action, and they committed atrocities against their own people every bit as bad as the Sandinistas. But anything was better than having communism right in his own backyard, he reasoned, so why not make a bundle in the name of the Stars and Stripes?

He had been out of the U.S. Army Special Forces too long, he told himself. Even with three tours of duty during America's longest and costliest war behind him and a host of decorations that proved his bravery in the face of enemy fire, Ellis still hadn't been prepared for this kind of action. And only three people even knew about his venture into Nicaragua. His wife—who had pleaded with him not to throw away his career at the university and go in search of "God knows what," as she had put it. The Man from Langley—his contact and go-between, who had promised him a quick two-month foray into Central America, where he was to nail down the legwork for the massive arms shipment to the Contra rebels, train them for another month, then go home to his wife and kids and the university. And an old Special Forces buddy from his Vietnam days—a man he just happened to stumble across in the Bahamas en route to Nicaragua and allude to that soldier what he was up to.

He hadn't even been in Managua two days, Ellis thought, and his cover had been blown by an ARDE defector. But something else must have happened for him to have been taken down so fast, so hard. Somebody was there in Nicaragua who had advance information about the arms shipment. Who? Names had been thrown around during his interrogation, but this wasn't his first stint in Nicaragua and Ellis knew you needed a scorecard to keep track of all the players. It could have been anybody who had set him up. Maybe even the Man from Langley.

"*Buenos días*, Major. I trust you are enjoying your stay with us?"

So lost had he been in pessimistic thought and pitying his own suffering, that Major Ben Ellis hadn't seen Comandante Bonano move into the cell. Silently, Ellis cursed the Sandinista with the shark's-teeth necklace. Bonano was always smiling, like he knew something no one else did, and that broad pearly white smile never failed to infuriate Ellis. Bonano was a slightly built man, and Ellis knew he could tear the Sandinista a new asshole—if only he could get his hands on him.

Bonano appeared to be alone, as he stood just inside the moss-slickened stone archway. *Zone Numero Uno*, as Bonano called the garrison and its perimeter, was the Sandinista version of the Russian gulag, and the comandante ran the hellhole like a gestapo death camp. Cell after cell was chock full of dissidents, counterrevolutionaries, CIA spooks, campesinos, and even a Catholic priest and a nun, what were known as *desaparecidos*, disappeared persons. That was the way it went in this country, Ellis knew. One day you're walking among your family or worrying about the Sandinistas seizing your farm and property or wondering where your next meal is coming from, and the next thing you know you're snatched away in the middle of the night if it was suspected that you were against the present powers-that-be.

Bonano began pacing around the cell, hands clasped behind his back. The smile vanished, replaced by a tight solemn expression.

"The Fat Man, hombre."

"What?"

"The Fat Man. Who is he and what is he doing here in Nicaragua. Tell me, *por favor*."

The same old song and dance. Repeatedly, Ellis had been asked who the Fat Man was during his torture.

"I told you before, I don't know any Fat Man."

"*Por favor*, hombre, do I need to refresh your memory of what has happened during your stay in lovely Nicaragua?"

"No, Comandante, I wouldn't want to damage the good thing I got going here."

Bonano chuckled. "*Yanqui* arrogance in the face of death. Let me explain something to you, Major. As of this morning we captured the armada of CIA gunships you had worked so hard to get in here. Of course, your fellow advisers were also most helpful in breaking the codes and radio frequency of that armada so that they believed everything was going down smoothly and that their landing zone was secure. I am here to tell you, it did not go down smoothly—for them. Now, I have more *yanquis* than I know what to do with. More mouths to feed. More screams for you to hear in the night."

Ellis felt the iceball lodge in his guts. He recalled hearing the screams of his fellow advisers during the night, screams that pierced the darkness like living things then were silenced by the chatter of AK47 autofire.

"Our plan in this zone," Bonano went on, "is fairly simple, but the CIA, crawling around the countryside like the *zompopo*, the red leaf-eating ants of the Matagalpa region, complicate our operations as they chew and bite at our outposts from the borders. *Sí*, they are like bothersome insects, but we will exterminate them in due course. We intend to drive every CIA adviser, every *yanqui merce-nario* and their Contras out of this region, even if that means bombarding the local villages with rockets and dislodging them from their entrenchments, hand-to-hand, house-to-house."

"With a little help, of course, from your friends, the Russians and the Cubans, who are known to be amassing their own death squads right here in the zone."

"You think you are clever, Major. You think your intelligence network is above corruption, that your information is ironclad. Many of your people are simply adventurers, perhaps like yourself, down here to strut around like peacocks and make some quick dinero. The Russians and the Cubans are necessary evils. They help us because they believe we will feel indebted to them, but they will also discover, soon, that they are not welcome here. If they would merely supply us with arms and equipment and keep their ambitions out of our country, if you and your fellow countrymen would leave Nicaragua, El Salvador, Honduras, and Costa Rica, leave Nicaragua and its problems to us, we would solve our problems in short time."

"How? By killing off tens of thousands of peasants who only want to be left alone, who only want a little piece of land to farm, who only want to educate, clothe, and feed their children?"

"It is not that simple. And who, Major, are the death squads? Your Contras have been known to slaughter villages, execute campesinos they suspect of having, ah, Marxist ideology."

"I don't answer for a few rogues."

"Bad apples, bad mangoes, *sí*. There are more than a few of them here in Nicaragua. But, Major, one man's terrorist is another man's freedom fighter. Now . . . this was just taken. Look. Tell me who he is. This is the Fat Man."

Ellis found himself looking at a 10x12 black-and-white pic of an enormously fat man in olive drab fatigues. The Fat Man was no misnomer. Puffing a fat stogie, probably Cuban, and looking like he owned the whole damn country. The Fat Man. Now Ellis knew exactly who Bonano was talking about. Ex–United States Army Colonel Hank Tilton. Ellis knew of the guy, had seen pictures and read

stories about him in American merc rags. Having become a
hardened cynic in his old age, Ellis didn't believe a damn
thing the American media, and that included all forms of
journalism, ever printed or poisoned television and radio
airwaves with. Everything was propaganda where Uncle
Sam had vested interests, and a man had to see it first then
make up his own mind. Ellis always made up his own mind
about events, and he had to admit he wasn't all that sure
who were the good guys and who were the bad guys
anymore in Central America. What Ellis had gathered from
trusted sources about Tilton was that the ex-colonel was just
a fat redneck from Alabama who held the people of Central
America in contempt and was down there to turn a buck.
He was typical, Ellis thought, of a lot of the brass down
there in Nicaragua looking to turn Central America into
another Vietnam for profit and decorations and to promote
floundering careers. They could kick up a bunch of shit
within commuting range, be back at the officers' club at
Fort Bragg in three hours, sipping cocktails and exchanging
war stories.

"Major, you could save yourself a lot of unnecessary
pain by simply telling me what you know about the Fat
Man. What we know is that he is here, in the zone, and he
is arming and training his own Contra force."

Ellis yielded to Bonano. "All right, all right. What I
know isn't much. I know his name is Hank Tilton. Army
colonel. Retired. I would imagine he is one of those types
you see a lot of down here, an adventurer looking to make
a big haul of *cordobas*. Maybe he works for the CIA, I don't
know, that's the rumor. Anything else . . . I don't know, I
couldn't tell you. That's it, I don't know anything else."

Bonano nodded several times. "I see."

"I'm not sure you do."

"What is that supposed to mean, hombre?"

"It means I'm telling ya I don't know what the fuck this
guy, the Fat Man, is really doing down here."

Bonano's gaze slitted. "But you can find out. You see,
I have plans for you, Major, big, big plans. Me and you
together, we will be a team. You will do some intelligence
gathering for me."

"And if I don't?"

Bonano cocked his head toward the doorway. "Ramon! Pedro!"

Shadows beyond the doorway. Scuffling. Something heavy.

"If you don't, Major . . ."

Ramon and Pedro appeared in the doorway, suddenly, out of nowhere it seemed. What appeared even more suddenly were the dozens of severed heads, set free from burlap sacks, that were rolling up at the major's feet. The scream lodged in Ellis's throat, and he felt the icy hand of fear on his neck.

"Anyone who does not prove himself useful to me, Major," Bonano said, laughing, drawing his finger across his throat. "These are many of your comrades who came with you here to Nicaragua, Major. Should you not help me, many more of them will die. Needlessly. Think about it. I would say that all of you are in over your heads?"

Sightless eyes stared up at Ellis, and he kicked several of the heads away. Ellis heard Bonano's laughter ringing in his ears as he swept out of the cell. *Crazy bastard! I gotta get outta here! I gotta get home!*

Suddenly his sedentary life back in the States looked very acceptable, and for once in his life, he wished he had listened to his wife.

Chapter 3

Lolita Armandez had heard the news. She was anxious, but feared the moment of truth. It would arrive soon enough, and when it did, how would she react? Was it, could it really be true what the villagers had said? They spoke in hushed but excited tones all around her about "Comandante Gringo," and his three *mercenarios*. A black one, a white-haired one, and a big one with a Germanic accent. In her mind, there was no mistaking who Comandante Gringo was.

No doubt at all. The lack of doubt made her even more afraid of the near future.

They had come to the Mosquito Coast, bearing weapons and supplies for the fighting unit of *El Tigre*. And *El Tigre*'s unit had marched off into the jungle more than two weeks ago to greet Comandante Gringo and escort him safely to the village. Supplies and weapons and Comandante Gringo had been transported further inland by the three Huey gunships on loan to *El Tigre* from the CIA. It was the relief *El Tigre* had hoped for, and now the fighting unit would be able to match the firepower of Bonano, who was known in the region as Attila the Hun for his savagery and cruelty against the campesinos. Even with the new supplies and armament, *El Tigre* and his men were still outnumbered and outgunned by Attila and his Sandinistas, but now they would stand a fighting chance.

Standing outside the doorway of her thatch-roofed hut, she looked around the village and felt her heart grow heavy. Everywhere stretched the ruins of the war. She bled inside for all of them, especially the young, the innocent victims of

14

war. The village was like one massive refugee camp. Old women and children, sitting in the shade of squalor and rubble, dreading the next raid. Fires roasting pigs and cattle, to be devoured by the hungry mouths of fighting men. Filthy, emaciated mongrels trotting through the dust under clouds of mosquitoes. Armed men, on edge, and waiting to engage the Sandinistas, who could attack the village at any time. Like herself, the village had seen and felt the ravages of war, as had all of Nicaragua. Long ago, what seemed like a hundred years ago, she had been a young woman, not quite twenty, full of hope and dreams for her country. She had been beautiful, sought after by every man in the village, but the war had frayed her beauty, given her a hard world-weary look, and worn her soul down so that she merely felt like a shadow of her former self. She was still a woman, but she had become a warrior, and she was expected to pull her own weight on the field of battle. She was tall, still lean, and long-legged, with full breasts and a sculpted face that could have belonged to a Mayan princess, but her dark eyes reflected the suffering she had seen and felt since the days when she had known and loved Comandante Gringo like no other man since.

She wondered, if the rumor was true, how she would greet him. Bitter? Angry that he had left her so suddenly? Or would the old fire still burn in her heart when she looked into his eyes? He was a man, after all, a real man, and he was the only man who had ever had that effect on her. He had been the father of their son.

Green bandanna wrapped around her mane of long raven black hair, she stared at the surrounding lumps of jungle foliage, squinted against the burning sky, and listened to the buzz of insects and the shriek of the howler monkeys. From somewhere in the village a baby cried. She felt the eyes of Hildago the Miskito boring into her from across the plaza. Father Escobarian and his nuns tended to those who had recently been wounded while securing the village perimeter against an attack by the hated Sandinistas. The town church, with so many gaping holes inflicted by mortar barrages, stood like a giant broken skeleton; only the belfry and the huge stone cross atop it remained undamaged. She shucked the AK47 higher up on her shoulder.

This, she knew, was a time of war, a time to stay hard to feelings, and not melt like some silly schoolgirl when Comandante Gringo arrived, bearing food and supplies for the villagers as if he were some savior of the Contra cause. But why? Why had he returned? To help fight the Sandinistas? Surely there was more to it? Had he returned to see her? And how would he take the news?

The news that they had had a son. So long ago. A son who no longer existed. Another life claimed by the war. Should she even tell him?

Lolita saw the Hippie come running up to her, his bearded face flushed with excitement. Hippie was the American free-lance journalist, a glory seeker who was there in Nicaragua to write articles and perhaps gather the research for a big book that would make him rich. She despised such men, who would seek fortune from the suffering of her people. The expensive camera equipment and tape recorder hung from the Hippie's skinny frame would cost a fortune in *cordobas* alone.

She thrust her hands on her hips as the Hippie rolled up in front of her. "*Qué?*"

"I suppose you've heard the news, señorita? Comandante Gringo and his mercenaries are on the way. The scouts saw *El Tigre* and his men moving down the trail to the north, only a few kilometers away. They should be here anytime. You can just feel the excitement in the air, can't you? Hope. New life. There may be hope for this zone yet, what with the arrival of Comandante Gringo, maybe he can help drive Attila out of the zone. By the way, is it true what the villagers say?"

"What is true?"

He took out his pad and pen, licked his lips. "That you had a son by Comandante Gringo?"

Her hand grabbed the Hippie's long hair as quickly as a snake would strike from the bush. She pulled the Hippie to his knees, baring her teeth in a snarl. He clawed at her hand, crying out in pain.

"Hey! What are you . . . dammit, you're hurting me!"

Lolita shook the Hippie like a wet dog. "You haven't seen hurt yet. Understand something, hombre. My affairs are my own business. They are not for some scribbler's memoirs. They are not for you or anyone else to sensationalize. Someday you will be gone from here with your big story to make a lot of money, while we are still here, fighting and dying. You are like a flea on the backs of the villagers, so I suggest you learn your place here and keep it." She flung the Hippie to the dirt and watched him crab away on his haunches.

He stood, slapping the dirt off his tiger-striped camos. "Hey, I didn't mean nothing. You don't have to kick me around like some dog. Jesus, I'm sorry, I'm sorry, all right."

"Be sorry somewhere else," Lolita Armandez growled, then walked into her hut.

To be alone.

To wait for Comandante Gringo.

Lieutenant Sergei Belikov spotted the Contra patrol as the column of armed men and their pack mules wended its way through the jungle trail. They appeared to be headed for a small clearing near the edge of the jungle for a rest. His own patrol party had tracked them for miles along the ridges of the hills to the north. One hundred Contra rebels led by the four mercenaries. Everything was set for the ambush.

Belikov rose from his prone position along the ridge and jerked a nod at Lieutenant Viktor Tomishta. Quickly, sweating heavily beneath the blazing sun, Tomishta ran up beside Belikov. Their squad of rebels remained outstretched along the ridge, awaiting orders to move out and close the pincer assault on the rebels in the valley below.

"Down there, comrade," Belikov said, and pointed.

Tomishta looked through the field glasses. "It is as we suspected. *Da, da,* I see them. And the four American mercenaries. Should I inform Major Kubchkin?"

"*Da.* He wants to attack the column, but he may also want us to capture the mercenaries and *El Tigre.*"

"*Da*, I understand. The arms shipment. It is fair game for anyone at this point."

The region, Belikov knew, was under heavy CIA intrusion. That morning it was reported that a fleet of CIA gunships, loaded down with armament for the Contras, had been shot down and its payload captured by the zone's comandante, Miguel Horchiba Bonano. Both sides were going to be scrambling, he thought, to get their hands on that payload. No one had a solid claim to that hardware yet.

"Our informant," Belikov told Tomishta, "reports that the American mercenaries brought with them a substantial haul of weapons, supplies, and medicine for *El Tigre*'s force, and have ingratiated themselves with the enemy. Enough new hardware to upscale hostile activities against Bonano. Ask the major when we should attack the column and how we should proceed with the attack."

Tomishta nodded and left Belikov alone on the ridge.

Belikov looked through the field glasses, grunting to himself. It would be very dangerous and very costly to current SPETSNAZ operations, he knew, if they were discovered actively engaged in the war in Nicaragua by the CIA. Still, they were under orders by Moscow to do something in the zone, balance the scales of war decisively in favor of the Sandinistas. Like the good soldier for the motherland that he was, Lieutenant Belikov intended to carry those orders out. To the bitter end. To the death.

Colonel Hank Tilton, formerly of the United States Army, now a free-lance mercenary, hated Nicaragua. He hated the peasants, the jungle, and the damnable mosquitoes and constant sweating. He hated anything that even remotely stank of Central America, but he was there on what he called a "miracle mission." And he was the miracle man. He would bet a batch of his finest Cuban cigars on that.

From atop the ridge of the heavily forested southern hills, he watched through high-powered Zeiss binoculars as the Contra column stopped near the edge of the jungle. Sentries immediately took up positions while the bulk of that force began sipping from their canteens. They were resting on their asses, he thought, unaware of the danger all around them. *Mangoes ready to be plucked.*

A wad of chewing tobacco pushed out Tilton's bulbous cheek. He wiped the sweat off his brow, spat, and hitched his khakis higher up over his enormous belly.

"This oughta be real interesting, boys. Real interesting, indeed."

"How's the valley shaping up, Colonel?"

Grinning, Tilton checked his mercenaries. Six mercs. Rosco. Lucas. Paneras the Panamanian. Jocko. Stilts. Willard the Beast. Six more hardened mercs waited at base camp at the foothills, securing their rear. They didn't look like much, he thought, twelve guns in all down there to tackle small armies, but they were equipped with enough firepower to take on Cuba if Castro's flunkies hit the shores of the Mosquito Coast.

"That Contra patrol is taking a little siesta. Dumbasses don't even know they got a small army of Somoza's finest looking right over their shoulders. Looks like we got us an ambush coming up, boys," Tilton said, and slid back from the ridge line to melt into the cool shade of the jungle canopy. He swatted at a mosquito, cursing viciously. "What we do is we wait and see how it goes down, then we move in and mop up. Could be some CIA assholes among that bunch and I'd like to take 'em alive. Remember what we're here for."

Willard the Beast, a huge, bald-headed, barrel-chested man with an M60, chuckled. "A cool million in cash, courtesy of the CIA. Right-o, Colonel man. How we gonna forget that. I go to sleep at night counting bills in my head and wake up counting where I left off."

"We ain't got it yet, boy," Tilton growled, squishing tobacco across the trail, where it splatted a small green lizard scaling a tree, knocking it into the brush. "Word I got from my man in Managua is that the comandante of this zone, one Bonano the Banana Man, or as the locals affectionately call him, Attila the Hun, is sitting on that stash right this minute over in that garrison we seen. Hell, he might not even know what he's sitting on. Stands to reason one of his flunkies might have found that stash in that Herc and could have taken off into the jungle by now. AWOL and filthy rich, looking to exchange all that green for a mountain of *cordobas*. Dunno. But we're gonna find out. Somehow. Someway. That's why we're down here. Bottom line. To make usselves rich men, the world's highest-paid soldiers of fortune."

Jocko, a tall, whip-thin merc with a full black beard, spoke up. "Problems getting our hands on that stash might've just started."

"How's that, boy?"

"The CIA is gonna be pissed," Jocko explained, "when they find out they lost that whole shipment, not to mention a cool million that fell into the wrong hands. They'll send somebody down here and they won't be a bunch of college boys on a panty raid either."

"Fuck that, and fuck them. Look at it like this," Tilton said, spat, "we're doing our country a service by going after that money and getting it back. I don't give a damn if we gotta raid that garrison usselves and level the friggin' place. If there's another way, I'll figure it out. Maybe a prisoner. Maybe some valuable intelligence that Banana can use. We'll do something. Right now, we wait and see how this firefight goes. Where's my bottle of Jack?"

Jocko threw Tilton his bottle of Jack Daniel's. The Fat Man took a healthy swig. He looked at the bottle, said, "Jocko, you better back off this shit. I don't need my boys all liquored up when the shit hits the fan, understand."

Jocko grumbled something, and the Fat Man scowled.

Tilton returned to watching the Contra patrol through his field glasses.

"Now, boys," the colonel muttered to himself, "let's get this show on the road. Uncle Tilt here is counting on you, all of you, to rack me up a nice little body count. Make life just a little easier for Uncle Sam's finest. You bloody no-good spic bastards! I'll stuff the Monroe Doctrine down your friggin' throats!"

Chapter 4

Vietnam taught Vic Gabriel that the jungle is neither friend nor foe. It is neutral, but it is not indifferent to the intrusion of man. Like anything else in life, it is how you use something that matters, Gabriel believed. An object, such as a gun or a knife, is neither good nor evil until it is touched by human hands. The jungle, the ex–Special Forces warrior knew, was likewise neither good nor evil. It can camouflage movements, allow a soldier to melt into invisibility and use it to his advantage, or it can swallow you alive. But wherever man lurks in the jungle, a new dimension is added.

The threat of sudden violence and swift death.

Like Vietnam, the jungles of Nicaragua were alive with the similar danger of the unseen enemy. In Nam, the VC. There, in Nicaragua, the Sandinistas. The ex–Special Forces warrior had learned to listen for certain sounds, certain movements, or lack of sound and movement in the jungle, to get a feel for danger or lack of danger.

Sensing some unknown presence in the surrounding jungle, he scoured the teeming nests of vines and foliage, searching for anything, but saw nothing except the Contra sentries moving off into the gloom to stand guard and seal a defensive perimeter while the rest of *El Tigre*'s force rested from the grueling two-day march. Men smoked cigarettes, or ate rice and cold beans from cans, or checked weapons. No one talked and certainly no one closed his eyes. Only the soft braying of pack mules or the frequent shriek of a howler monkey broke the heavy pall of silence around the camp.

Gabriel fired up a Marlboro with his engraved Zippo as Johnny Simms, Henry van Boolewarke, and Bad Zac Dillinger joined him. Mentally, he chewed over the situation. Although he wasn't one to delve into the politics of any situation, particularly the controversial ideology of the Nicaraguan disaster, Vic Gabriel believed in certain basic human rights. In Nicaragua, it was freedom versus oppression, and it was that cut-and-dried, although the Soviets and their Cuban lackeys, and to some extent, the CIA had muddied up the already messy political and military situation in the largest but most sparsely populated of the Central American countries. But he wasn't there to choose sides, even though he'd chosen the side of the lesser of two evils—the Contras. All in all, history in Central America had created and proven the "pistolero effect." Simply meaning one reigning fascist regime was overthrown and replaced by another, and always at the expense of the peasant. Still, Gabriel believed, there is always hope that someday things will be different, will be better. That was the driving force as to why he and his commandos fought their wars. Deliverance unto hope.

Puffing on a fat Cuban stogie, Dillinger sidled up to Gabriel. "*El Tigre* says that village is only a handful of klicks further down the trail. Could be a bad thing to stop for a siesta now, VG."

Like Gabriel, all three of his commandos were decked out in dark green jungle camos, toting M16s with M203 grenade launchers, sheathed Ka-Bar knives, their webbing loaded down with a dozen frag grenades. The jungle steamed with heat, and shafts of bright sunlight knifed through the foliage; the four commandos were soaked with sweat. Boolewarke had his Barnett Panzer crossbow slung around his shoulder and a belted M60 by his side, and Dillinger had his twin ivory-handled .45 Colts hip-holstered for a quick cross draw.

"I hear ya, Bad One," Johnny Simms, the black commando from the mean streets of Washington, D.C., added. "Two days we been hiking through the jungle and not a peep from one Sandinista. Not even the hint of a recon patrol. Don't feel right. Somethin's in the air. Been too damn quiet for a country that's supposed to be at war."

"Smart move on your part," Henry van Boolewarke told Gabriel, abruptly changing the subject, "to keep your old contacts in Managua. Word got to *El Tigre* fast, and he was front and center at the beach to pick up our gifts, courtesy of our now-bulging war fund. These weapons and food and medicine we unloaded on them, you made sure they'd go the extra mile for us. Nice move. So far, so good."

"Coming here empty-handed with just the love of Jesus in our hearts for their cause," Gabriel said, "wouldn't have exactly endeared us to a bunch of guerrilla fighters using vintage World War II weapons to fight an army supported and financed by Mother Russia's finest. The Contras need all the help they can get, and for once we're in a position to help somebody financially besides ourselves."

"Be kinda like going to a BYOB party with no booze," Simms cracked, "then bumming drinks and grabbing your best buddy's girl by the ass."

"A bunch of Santa Clauses, we ain't," Dillinger growled, chomping on his stogie. "We're here for one thing and one thing only."

"That's right. I had a bad feeling when I talked to my old war buddy Major Ellis," Gabriel said. "My suspicions panned out. He's disappeared without a trace and word of that CIA arms shipment falling into Sandinista hands spread like wildfire. His wife hasn't heard from him in weeks and she asked me to do some digging, even though I intended to do that anyway. My guess is a worst-case scenario. Ellis is being held down here against his will, and the Sandinistas or the Russians or both intend to use him as a propaganda tool. If they did that, it would certainly give the edge to the Sandinistas, as far as world sympathy goes. American bullies, CIA covert activities and sabotage, and all that garbage, that would be a parade of shit-smearing Uncle Sam would never live down. No more support for the Contras on the American homefront, particularly if Congress gets wind that a massive secret arms shipment was made. Ellis would be tried and convicted back home before the first story broke in the *Washington Post*. Too many people believe what they read in newspapers and see on TV. Unfortunately, in some arenas, the pen is mightier than the sword, and the American media has a way of jumping on a bandwagon and beating something to death."

"Called propaganda," Dutch muttered.

"Called bullshit," Simms added.

"So, this is still a mercy mission?" Dillinger posed.

"We've all done the same thing for each other many times before," Gabriel said, blowing thick streams of smoke through his nostrils. "I owe Ellis. He saved me from certain death in Vietnam, and that's no propaganda. Our patrol was ambushed and wiped out by the VC. I was the only one left, shot to hell and bleeding to death before Ellis pulled me out of there, under heavy VC fire. I promised to square the tab. This is my chance. Besides, it's as good an opportunity as any to be a thorn in somebody's side down here."

Dutch grunted. "Like that Ivan presence that supposedly is being heated up down here."

"That, too," Gabriel said. "From what I could gather on the islands during these past few weeks, this whole country is like one big volcano ready to erupt. If Ivan is here in numbers as big as I've heard, then they're looking to upscale the war."

"Which means the return of William Walker and the marines," Dillinger said. "Or worse, an invasion by Uncle Sam."

"Possibly," Gabriel admitted.

A cynical frown shadowed Simms's face. "Just what the big Uncle needs. Another Nam. More domino-theory bullshit being kicked around by desk-jockey brass."

"It might not be such bullshit, Johnny boy," Dillinger said. "Nicaragua's only a stone's throw away from Mexico. I guess since the Russians reason that if we can be in Turkey, they can be in Central America, right in America's backyard. Suppose it makes sense from where they sit."

"Twisted sense," Boolewarke snarled. "If there are Ivans here, by God, I'll blow them right back into the Stone Age and they'll never wished they'd crossed the Atlantic in search of that big hammer-and-sickle springboard. I guess

Cuba's not enough for them, they want all of Central America. Rotten bastard pig farmers!"

"Comandante Gringo, amigos."

Gabriel found *El Tigre* front and center. The dark-skinned Nicaraguan had thick shoulder-length black hair, a full black beard. He toted one of the new M16s with M203 grenade launcher Gabriel had brought to the Mosquito Coast, and had a large machete sheathed by his side. He was a slightly built man, not much to look at, but Gabriel had watched *El Tigre* closely the past few days. And he could march with full gear through the jungle, swiftly, without a sound, like a ghost, and without complaint. He could go long distances, double time, without food and water, and not miss a stride, not even rattle the brush. The Nicaraguan was in top shape, knew the country, knew men, knew soldiering, and had that charismatic presence that is so essential when commanding troops on the field of battle. He would get right down there and do exactly what he asked of anybody else. He was respected among the ranks, and his word was like gold.

"May I join you?"

"What's up *jefe*?" Gabriel asked.

"A smoke, *por favor*?"

Gabriel gave *El Tigre* a Marlboro, lit it for him.

El Tigre squatted on his haunches, drawing easily on the smoke. "I have news for you. First, on behalf of my men and myself, I want to thank you again for the weapons and supplies you brought for us. This was most generous. It will not be forgotten."

Gabriel showed *El Tigre* an easy smile. "Can't fight a war with machetes and a tommy gun down to six rounds, guy."

"*Sí*. And the CIA, they are not always so dependable these days. That is what I wish to talk to you about."

Gabriel felt himself tense up. CIA. Plenty of bad experience with the CIA. He knew they were there in Nicaragua—hell, everywhere in Central America—and he needed those guys like he needed to catch AIDS. Time to get to the black heart of the grim matter.

"The arms shipment that fell into Bonano's hands?"

"*Sí*. But first, the man you came here looking for, our informant inside Bonano's camp says this Major Ellis is a prisoner at the garrison." *El Tigre* took a stick, swept aside some brush, and began drawing in the dirt. "We are here. Bonano, also known as Attila the Hun for his indiscriminate slaughter of the campesinos in this zone, his garrison is here, to the south, about fifteen kilometers from our present position. Your friend is being held there. He is still alive. The other CIA advisers who came with him have been executed, but not until they gave Bonano the codes he needed to lure in the C130s stocked with weapons."

"Weapons destined for *El Toro*," Zac Dillinger said, huffing out a thick cloud of cigar smoke. "Who we're supposed to be linking up with in this village, San Pedro."

A glint shone in *El Tigre*'s eyes. "Amigo, something I did not tell you—I am also *El Toro*. Those weapons were meant for my fighting unit."

Simms shook his head. "Man, you need a damn scorecard down here to keep track of all the players."

"It is necessary for me, amigo, to assume different identities, play different roles depending on the situation. Security reasons. I am the only real hope the Contras have in this zone. If I am captured or killed, there is no one—and I do not just pat myself on the back here—to fill these shoes. I have been fighting this war for ten years. I have seen plenty of death, and dealt plenty of death myself. I may not look scarred, but I have the soul of an old, old man. I'm sure you can see it in my eyes, as I see it in your eyes. There is rumor of something else you should know about."

Gabriel cocked an eyebrow, talking around his Marlboro. "Yeah. What's that?"

"The CIA sent funds with that shipment. Cash. One million dollars American. It was meant to keep our operations solvent, money meant to buy arms again and again and recruit and train new fighters for the counterrevolution."

"So now what you're saying," Dutch growled, "is that Attila's sitting on top of a cool million Yankee."

El Tigre-Toro shrugged. "What can I say, amigo? This

is a most serious development. We deal with it. We know for a fact that the CIA often comes down here with arms and large sums of cash to cut deals with the *narcotraficantes*. The Colombians. The Panamanians. The Bolivians. This is reality. Arms for drugs. It happens a lot. We have more to worry about than just war, we also have to contend with the greed of the drug traffickers. It is funny, indeed, how do you say, hypocritical? Your country claims to fight a war on drugs, yet planeloads of weapons are dropped off here in Nicaragua, then the same CIA planes fly back to the United States loaded down with cocaine and marijuana. One dirty hand washing the other. That is life. That is reality. Everyone but the Nicaraguan fighting for his life gets what he wants. The Nicaraguan, he gets death. The rogue CIA gangsters, they grow fat on our pain and dying. Drugs-for-arms supports the Contra effort, but this is something you will never hear about in your press."

"You're not telling me anything new," Gabriel said. "I've seen it more than once."

"Indeed. Now. You need not worry about the loyalty of my men, they will fight to the death and they will now follow you into hell, if that's what it takes to remove Attila from this zone and free your friend. You did us a favor with your arms cache and medicine and other supplies. The five hundred pounds of steaks was a nice touch," he said, smiling, "but do not spoil us. A well-fed soldier is often an unmotivated soldier, and a lazy soldier gets dead here quick. Anyway, in Nicaragua you will find that favors do not go unrewarded. Further, treachery does not go unpunished. There is much treachery down here. We have Cubans, Russians, the CIA to deal with, and at times we do not know who the real shadow men are. They come, they go. They kill, they make money off the suffering of Nicaragua. Each side claims to believe in a cause, whether Contra or Sandinista, but no one can ever be sure." *El Tigre* paused, blowing funnels of smoke out of flared nostrils. "You, you men are genuine. You came. You gave. You asked for nothing except for us to help you find your friend, a man you say you owe a blood debt to. I can respect that. I should have more comrades like you."

Gabriel had *El Tigre* measured. He was the real thing, and he would go the distance for a trusted ally. "Once we get Ellis out of that garrison, *El Tigre*, you're on your own."

El Tigre nodded. "*Sí*. I understand. This is perfectly acceptable. You leave when you have done what you came here to do."

"But if we can lighten your load along the way," Gabriel went on, "we will. That means racking up a fat body count of your enemies before leaving."

"This sounds good to me. *Sí*. With patriotism and God, we will defeat communism."

"Amen, amigo," Dutch growled, and won an approving smile from *El Tigre*.

Gabriel didn't know how to take that. When a man feels he has some divine intervention on his side working for him, he can do strange things. Catholicism was a huge moving force in Nicaragua, but a man can twist religion and warp it to suit his own purposes. Gabriel preferred to leave "God" out of it. Whatever Force created the tragicomedy called the human race, didn't exactly beam, Gabriel thought, when men set out to kill each other in the name of Right.

El Tigre looked up at the Afrikaaner. "I see you have a particular fierce hatred for the communists."

"Damn straight," Boolewarke rasped. "They only took everything I had in this world. Burned my ranch. Murdered my people."

El Tigre nodded. "That is much the same way it is here. The Sandinistas, backed with their Marxist ideology, seize farmland, murder the peasants in the name of reform. This translates into a dictatorship, where a few have and most have to worry about where their next meal is coming from."

"So, you'll understand," the ex–Recces commando added, "if you see me going a little overboard on some Ivans. The only thing I'll go overkill on is something that stinks of Little Mother Russia."

El Tigre nodded, several times. "My family, my wife and three children, they were murdered by the communists. My farm was seized by the state. I was forced to flee the country and hide out in Costa Rica for two years. That was until I hooked up with the CIA and they helped me form my own fighting unit. Many were of Somoza's national guard, but down here, who knows, a man can change sides and shape his own ideology depending on his situation at the moment."

"Speaking of fighting units," Dillinger said, "anybody seen the guys we're supposed to be fighting lately?"

"They are everywhere, amigo. And they are nowhere. I sense you do not like the quiet. I understand. When it is too quiet like this—"

Autofire raked the air in long blistering chatters. Screams cut through the jungle.

"Emboscada! Emboscada!"

"Looks like Somoza's finest," Dutch hollered, unslinging his M16, "found us instead!"

Gabriel and his commandos were up and running for cover. Foliage was chewed apart as locust swarms of hot ComBloc lead sizzled the air. Contras were dropping all up and down the trail, blood gouting from fist-sized wound canals. Deep in the jungle, Gabriel made out the figures, scrambling through the gloom, firing on the run.

And the ex–Special Forces warrior saw the enemy converging on the trail from behind. They were pinned down, hemmed in.

Chilling screams ripped the air as men died.

And for a moment, Vic Gabriel went back. To a time when something like this had happened, long, long ago. In another world. Another hell. Another ambush.

Guerrilla warfare, but a different face on the enemy.

It could have been déjà vu, he thought, hearing the screams of the wounded and the dying all around him as lead ripped through the vines above his face. It took him back to a point in time that had, inadvertently, led him to Nicaragua.

Chapter 5

Nineteen-year-old Vic Gabriel knew he was dying. Three days away from his twentieth birthday, and he was thousands of miles away from home, his life seeping out through the holes in his upper chest and side, a soldier alone, dying in the jungles of Southeast Asia. Three days away from some much-deserved R&R in Saigon. Three days away from just collapsing in the warm, waiting arms of his girl, Ana Nua Phyun, and idling a few days away in her bed, drinking, loving, maybe looking at a future with her back in the World. Three days—an eternity. Three days he might not ever see. No, he didn't see his life passing before his eyes, something he'd heard about that happened to men when they were at the edge of eternity. No, he just wanted to survive, to live to see this night through, to feel the sunshine of tomorrow warm his face. To see his father. To see his girl.

To find the bastard that had set him and his squad up for this ambush.

Tomorrow might never come.

He crawled through the bush, clinging to consciousness through sheer iron will, and motivated by fear to kill the enemy. No despair, no surrender, he told himself. He had to live. He had to. His life was worth something, had to be. He believed in fate, destiny, and this simply wasn't his time. Or was it? Too much to do, too much to live for, but nobody wants to die, and what the hell makes him any better than his buddies who had already been slaughtered on that trail? What the hell made him so special that fate might step in and save his ass? He'd certainly been right

there when the first wall of bullets had collapsed over them.
He'd been one of the first ones hit and knocked on his ass,
tasting his own blood as it washed over his face, and
Charlie had swarmed over them, a flood tide of screaming
human rage.

That seemed like a hundred lifetimes ago now. A
hundred dead men since.

Fire raced through his body, and every time he
breathed it was pure white-hot agony. He guessed at least
three VC slugs had passed through his side, shattering ribs.
He was alive, though, but the men of his squad, all eight of
them, were dead and strewn up and down the trail, a
bloody carpet of tangled limbs and leaking guts. Charlie
had claimed the night. But how? It was almost as if they
knew they were coming, almost as if they knew every step
they were taking on this search-and-destroy. They had been
waiting, and they had opened up and mowed them down,
hardened Green Berets who had walked into hell before
and come back to tell about it. Not this time. Not ever
again.

And Fire Support Base Dragon was thirty-five klicks
or more away. Somewhere. Somewhere back in the jungle.
Hell, he didn't know where. All he knew was that he was
inside the Cambodian border, bleeding to death, and yeah,
maybe, just maybe wondering what the hell he was dying
for after all.

He could hear the rustle of the brush around him.
Charlie was out there. Stalking. Coming for him. This was
his first behind-the-lines killhunt without his father. Dad,
he heard his mind cry, I've let you down. I don't know if I'm
coming back . . . don't know . . .

He thought about his father. Somewhere back in the
World. Called back two days before this search-and-
destroy. By Saunders. Saunders, the CIA shadow man,
who had arranged this mission. Saunders, he was sure, was
behind this disaster. But why? Why? Was he dying so some
renegade CIA shadow man could cover his ass? Keep all the
dirt from covering some covert CIA operations that dealt in
gunrunning and heroin? The truth was there about this
Saunders, and both Gabriels had suspected Saunders was

doing a little illicit moonlighting profiteering from the war. Both Gabriels had caught glimmers of the light of the real truth. Saunders was dirty, and he knew it, and he knew that both Gabriels knew it. So why continue to deal with Saunders? Because the CIA and some top brass had ordered both Gabriels to go with the program. That was Vietnam. Dirty. Treacherous. Corrupt. What was this domino theory? It was bullshit. The only guys that counted were the grunts who were there fighting to stay alive and make it back home. It was a rare occasion when you could tell the good guys from the bad guys when it came to the CIA and the big brass. Somebody somewhere was lining their pockets off the blood and suffering of the average grunt. It was all bullshit, it was all some politician's dream. But he had a job to do, and that was to seek out and engage the enemy. And, yeah, make it back home.

Suddenly, the sky above the jungle canopy was lit up by flares. Vic Gabriel looked up, squinting against the fire in the sky. They were closing. They were coming for him.

He heard the growl. Found himself staring right into the fierce eyes of a tiger, not more than ten feet away. Even the whistling and crackling of flares, as fire and sparks rained down through the canopy, spooked the predator. One final growl, and the tiger melted into the darkness of the jungle.

Weapon. He needed a weapon. Something more than just the Ka-Bar sheathed on his hip. He looked down, and froze for a moment. His hands had sunk into the pile of mush that had been the stomach of his buddy, Cummings, from Omaha, Nebraska. Cummings. His second tour of duty. His last. Cummings the guy who could find humor under the worst of situations and make you laugh. Who kept it light and going. Cummings who wouldn't make anybody laugh ever again.

No time to bleed for the dead. Dammit! And just who the hell were the good guys anyway? Saunders, you bastard! Was this some way for Saunders to shave the odds? One Gabriel down, one to go. He wasn't about to die. Not now. Not ever. If he was going to die there, then he would take as many VC with him as he could. Fuck medals.

*Fuck the mission. Fuck Saunders. If anybody had written
his ass off, they were going to find out how big a mistake
they had made.*

Then they came.

*Shadows, silent. Dark faces, eyes wild and lit by the
glare of raining fire.*

Adrenaline pumping through him, young Vic Gabriel
swept up the belted M60. Some berserker rage fevered his
brain, as he pulled back the trigger and screamed, "Come
on, you bastards! Taste some of this! Come on, motherfuck-
ers!"

They came at him, and they dropped where they
surged from the jungle. Five, six, a dozen, he wasn't sure.
They spun, they screamed, they piled up on dead Green
Berets they had massacred a hundred lifetimes ago. He just
kept firing, spent shell casings twirling around his mask of
demonic fury, the roar of the spitting man-eater ripping
into his eardrums. Teeth gritted, he stood, raking the jungle
with relentless machine-gun fire, shearing foliage, splitting
the night asunder with the screams and death gurgles of the
VC. As they fell, he retreated. The world spun. Bile
bubbled and burned into his throat.

He padded deeper into the jungle. Stumbled. It was
close to dawn, and he could see the sky lighten up ahead,
through a break in the jungle.

A clearing.

There was some dark behemoth structure, like a
temple of some kind in the distance. Buddha. A religious
shrine, he thought, that would see his death, or his glory.

He trudged across the clearing, determined to make
his last stand at the Buddhist temple. They were behind
him. They were all around him. He could hear the rapid-
fire chatter of Vietnamese. Angry voices cutting through
the murky gloom of encroaching dawn.

The wall of jungle around the temple was like a ring of
sentinels in his sight, wavering, onrushing, then receding in
his eyes. His body screamed with pain, and he felt the
blood, sticky and warm, soaked into his khakis, ingrained,
it seemed, in his flesh.

He started to stumble up the stone steps. He heard

*them. Could feel them massing behind him, just yards away
across the stretch of no-man's-land.*

Dead man's land.

*He fell, and cracked his head against stone, stars and
white light exploding in his eyes. He looked up, and saw the
mammoth statue of Buddha, grinning, it seemed, right
down into his face. Cursing. Laughter.*

*The sky seemed to part with some distant noise, a
bleating sound, that filled his brain and raked his agony
with hot needles.*

*Nineteen-year-old Vic Gabriel turned around, and saw
the shadows charge from the jungle, weapons blazing.*

It happened to him once in a while. It was the closest
thing to an hallucination he would ever experience. Even as
the bullets chewed the foliage around him, and the Sandinistas surged through the jungle trying to take his life as
violently and as quickly as possible, he had to pull himself
back from the past with a sheer effort of will. Traumatic
experience, he knew, can do that to the human mind. A life
without trauma, though, a life without tragedy, is a life not
worth living. When everything is too easy, too cut-and-
dried, a man never finds himself, never has to dig, eat shit,
and suck it up. He never really knows what he's made of.
Physically, mentally, you have to be pushed to the edge,
survive, and come back to see what's really inside. Your
sanity, your principles have to be tried and tested to the
breaking point in order for you to really see the world for
what it is, and see yourself as you really are. Vic Gabriel
believed this with all his heart. And he had been driven to
the edge, of death, and of insanity, more than once. To and
beyond the edge, and come back. The only limitations a
man has are the ones he imposes upon himself.

Trauma and tragedy, depending on how a man re-
groups from the experience, Gabriel believed, build and
solidify character. Even though they scar deep and forever,
they make a man what he is and allow him to face life
without fear, without regret. Even though they plant
images in his mind's eye for life, they have made him
stronger than whatever he was before.

Significant, or life-threatening events in a man's life, can shape images so strong, so vivid in his mind, that they can creep up suddenly, released by some present circumstance, set off by some present image, and then swarm over him and lock him inside his head for a moment. Sometimes a fatal moment.

In this case, the Nicaraguan jungle, the Sandinista ambush, had hurled Vic Gabriel back in time, years and years ago to where life had actually begun to form him into what he was in the present.

There was only one way to save the moment, Vic Gabriel knew. That was to lead a devil-be-damned charge into the jungle and take the fight into the heart of the enemy and cut their heart right out.

"Come on! Move out!" Gabriel hollered over the din of autofire. "*El Tigre!* Get 'em moving! Ahead!"

Led by Gabriel, his commandos, and *El Tigre*, the Contra counterattack took shape, fast and furious. To hesitate for a split second, Gabriel knew, is to die in such a situation. Already, dozens of *El Tigre*'s fighting men had been left dead by the initial enemy onslaught. And the screams of the horribly wounded shrouded the trail. Several pack mules, braying wildly, dropped under curtains of lead, bloody carcasses riddled by bullets. Still more Contras pitched in death throes to the trail. Utter chaos and confusion seized the moment, and Gabriel knew it was up to him to pave the way and seize back the moment, turn the tide.

Penetrating the jungle, Gabriel and Simms, side by side with *El Tigre*, triggered 40mm hellbombs from their M203s. Boolewarke and Dillinger stormed across the jungle trail, and led a desperate counterattack there, covering the rear of Gabriel's advancing spearhead. Dutch's M60 ripped free, and Dillinger hurled one grenade after another into the charging, shrieking Sandinistas. The entire jungle seemed lit by fire for eternal moments, and a ring of explosions sealed the Contras behind a wall of flames and smoke and flying limbs. Tremendous explosions scythed through the Sandinista charge, and seemed to stop them, cold and dead, in their tracks. As bits and pieces of mangled corpses spattered the foliage, the Sandinistas began to retreat, rushing back into smoke and fire, flying bark and a fluttering rain of shredded jungle canopy.

Gabriel knew it was time to turn it up a few notches. So did *El Tigre*, as he yelled, "Forward! Forward!"

The dead, the dying, and the wounded were left behind on the trail as the Contra fighting unit advanced, savagely hurling lead and hellbombs after the retreating enemy. Gabriel was pleased with the grim determination and unflinching resolve of the Contra fighting unit as they stalked the retreating enemy, but he and Simms had their own problems to deal with.

Shadows with flaming weapons leaped ahead of Gabriel and Simms, and they mowed those figures down with steady M16 autofire. Gabriel and Simms and *El Tigre* spent clip after clip as they ran through the jungle, stitching the spines and skulls of the enemy with long lethal lead sprays. Gabriel ignored the vines tearing at his fatigues, the sweat and blood pouring down his face.

"Get a prisoner!" the ex–Special Forces warrior hollered at *El Tigre*, who nodded that he understood.

They were soon to discover that the enemy wasn't going to allow themselves to be captured.

As they rolled up on the wounded enemy, Gabriel saw dying Sandinistas impale themselves on their machetes.

"What the hell?" Simms growled.

It froze Gabriel for a moment, too, as close to a dozen of the enemy numbers committed suicide. They slumped forward on machetes or stuck the muzzles of AK47s in their mouths and squeezed the triggers. It was a horror show, and Gabriel was momentarily stumped. Whatever enemy numbers had survived the retreat through the jungle were now climbing a hill beyond the green wall of tree line. They never made it to the ridge. Crouched in a neat row behind the trees, Contras cut loose with relentless autofire, sent those enemy numbers tumbling back down the hillside.

M16 low by his side, Gabriel walked up on one of the dead enemy who had impaled himself. With the steel-tipped toe of his combat boot, he flipped the corpse over on his side.

El Tigre walked up beside Gabriel. Johnny Simms moved out of the bush and joined the two men.

Gabriel stared down at the lifeless face, blood trickling down the sides of its mouth, mosquitoes already picking at dead flesh. "Interesting. I'll lay odds that this guy isn't any Sandinista. In fact, I'd bet my own personal savings back in Nassau that this guy is either a Russian or an East German."

A plan, shadowy in its conception, but taking shape more each moment, began to form in Colonel Hank Tilton's mind. He stood on the ridge, watching, listening to the death throes of the battle below in the valley. He spat a stream of tobacco juice. He was impressed with the large Contra fighting unit.

"Got me an idea, boys," Tilton told his men as they gathered around him. "Looks like we got four mercenaries of undetermined origin leading that Contra unit. Experienced fighting men."

"Yeah. They repulsed that ambush, damn near without blinking an eye, it looked like," Rosco said. "They're good. Moved right into it, without hesitating, rolled it up, flank to flank. Dropped a few dozen of those Sandinistas where they stood before Nicaragua's finest tucked tail and ran."

"Yeah, but somethin's telling me," Tilton said, "that we got other players in this scene."

"Who?" Jocko asked. "Russians? Cubans? East Germans?"

"Not sure, at this junction. Reports are that Ivan's in the zone," Tilton answered. "I'm thinking that somehow Bonano the Banana has got himself hooked up with outside forces here. I want to follow those boys down there. Wherever they go, we go. Somehow, we bag us one of those four *mercenarios* down there and use him or them to get us into Attila's camp." He looked at his troops, smiled, spat. "Boys, within the next few days, we're going to be rich men. We didn't come here for nothin' else but for that CIA wad, so let's stay focused, all right."

Colonel Hank Tilton stood there on the ridge, arms akimbo, and smiled. Easy pickings, he thought. Money in the bank.

And he was already counting up that CIA wad of dead presidents in his head. All the way out of Nicaragua and into the Bank of Nassau. After all, it was him out there, risking his ass, and, hell, the CIA didn't need all that money anyway.

As he looked at the wounded, stretched out along the trail, and listened to the groans and croaks of pain, Vic Gabriel thought, *Sometimes you get lucky. Sometimes that bullet with your name on it misses you by inches. Someday, I'm sure it will come for me, but not today, and not anytime soon if I have something to say about it.*

"We gotta move 'em out," Gabriel told *El Tigre* as they walked among the wounded.

"I have got eighteen seriously wounded on my hands," *El Tigre* informed Gabriel. "Fifteen are dead."

"How far is San Pedro?" Gabriel asked.

"Another six kilometers. But we must move through the valley. Open ground. Good ground for a sniper to pick off more of my soldiers."

"Not a good thing to leave ourselves exposed, not at all," Gabriel said, "but it has to be done."

Dutch was helping tend to the wounded, and Gabriel watched for a moment as the ex–Recces commando, who was also a paramedic, treated the wounds, bandaged them as best he could, Boolewarke instructing Contras on what to do.

Just then, Simms and Dillinger moved onto the trail, back from recon.

"Well?" Gabriel asked them.

"All quiet. No sign of any activity at the moment," Dillinger reported. "*El Tigre*'s men got the place sealed up in a defensive perimeter, just in case they come back."

"I will do as you instructed," *El Tigre* told Gabriel. "We will have our flanks and rear guarded on the way to San Pedro. How this happened—I can only say that we must have an informant in our camp."

Simms nodded, grunting. "Sure as hell stands to reason somebody among our ranks ain't on the level."

"Had to know we were coming," Dillinger added.

"Hell, we haven't seen the first hint of the enemy for days. All of a sudden they pop up, out of nowhere."

"Any chance of flushing this informant out?" Gabriel asked.

"There is always a chance," *El Tigre* answered.

"All right, we'll put the more seriously wounded on the pack mules and makeshift stretchers," Gabriel said. "Carry the rest, if they can't walk."

"Why?" Simms asked, shaking his head. "Why did those guys kill themselves instead of risk being captured?"

"They were under orders not to be captured," Gabriel said. "If they'd gone back, they would have been killed on the spot. This was meant to be a suicide attack."

"*Sí*," *El Tigre* offered. "That is Attila's way. If they could not kill us all, or bring him back prisoners, they would have to kill themselves. I have seen this before. It would be wise to retreat into Honduras and regroup . . . but we have come this far and we must fight Attila to the end, however it turns out. Besides, the Honduran government is putting pressure on us to leave their country and things are not as safe there as they were."

"But the Russians can set up camp in El Salvador?" Dillinger scoffed.

"That, amigo, is the sorry state of affairs down here. There are many sides fighting each other for control of Nicaragua, but many have neither just cause nor ideals, except to impose their own will on the Nicaraguans. As it has been, and sadly, as it shall perhaps continue to be. I fight for the common man, the peasant who is being trampled into the dust by the current regime."

Vic Gabriel scoured the shadowy recesses of the jungle all around him. They were out there, he knew, watching, waiting. Just like the VC. He felt himself freeze up for a second, his mind pulling him back.

"VG? You all right?"

Gabriel looked at Dillinger. "Yeah. I'm fine. I just don't want any more surprises. Okay, *El Tigre*, let's get this show on into San Pedro. Come nightfall, we're heading out. I want to get a good look at this garrison before we make our next move."

The cries of the wounded filtered through Vic Gabriel's mind. For some reason, he felt haunted, more haunted than he had felt in a long time.

They paid their ten cordobas at customs without argument or complaint. It seemed to Zac Dillinger that that was just the way business was done in Nicaragua—indeed, thievery, bribery, and usury were a way of life in all of Central America. If you're a norteamericano, they fleece you because they assume you're loaded with big Yankee dollars and it is their right to help themselves to those dollars because they are oppressed and downtrodden by Uncle. And if they can't lighten your billfold with their contrived rules and regulations or outright thievery, the private investigator from sunny Fort Lauderdale thought, they'll put you in a position where you're forced to bribe them. If you can't pay, you sit in jail, or worse. If a man is foolish enough to complain or argue with this unwritten but universally acknowledged custom, life becomes very difficult in the lower Americas and one is usually never heard from again. Dillinger knew. This was his third trip to Central America and every time he was lucky enough to go back to the States he was generally broke. But at least he had lived to tell about it each time. So far.

Not that Dillinger and Simms were smuggling any contraband into Nicaragua in their large black duffel bags, but they were there in the country on grim business. They were dressed in khakis and combat boots, sported dark shades and expensive Rolex watches. The wary observer, and there were plenty of them in Nicaragua two years after the revolution, would spot them for what they were. If ever two men looked like soldiers of fortune, the granite-faced, white-haired man and his stocky black buddy stood out in the throngs of passengers in the terminal of Augusto C. Sandino International Airport like a couple of Wall Street suits in Harlem.

"I tell ya, Bad One," Johnny Simms said as they plowed along with the cattle surge of Latinos, businessmen, and all ilk and strain of foreign tourists down the terminal, "I don't know how I let you talk me into this. I could be back in

Miami with my little chiquita right now, soaking up sun by the shore and sipping on those tall funny drinks with the umbrellas in 'em. Coming down here on your buddy's request to mix it up with Contras and Sandinistas, ducking KGB and CIA bullets alike, ain't exactly my idea of some R&R. Not just that, but your buddy's using go-betweens to get your ass down here. You haven't even heard personally from this guy, Gabriel, not word one. I don't like it. Somethin' feels real wrong. I smell somethin'."

"What are you whining about anyway?" Dillinger gruffed. "You got paid ten grand up front and you'll get another ten grand at the end of the month. That'll buy you plenty of chiquitas and all the R&R a man can stomach in Miami, Johnny boy."

"Yeah, if I live that long."

Dillinger's gaze turned solemn as he slowed his strides and looked out onto the runway through the terminal glass. He couldn't even begin to count the numbers of military aircraft lined up on the runway. Gunships and transport planes, surrounded and guarded by heavily armed uniformed soldiers of the Sandinista People's Army. Everything out there was smoked over by haze and the burning glare of a fierce sun. This was, indeed, a country on fire, he decided.

"Look at that, will ya. How much Russian hardware you think is out there, Johnny boy? How many Company goons you think Uncle's got down here? And how many hard-bitten, down-on-their-luck mercs like us come down here looking for a little dough or a little adventure so they can go home and flex their muscles at the neighborhood bar? Christ. This is a country at war, tugged and kicked around by the superpowers, the Eagle and the Bear, clawing and scratching at each other to claim another piece of turf for their flag. This is just a country of peasants who only want a little land to farm, a decent education for their kids, and a little luck to be able to see the next sunrise. And all the foreign guns roll in here to try to tell 'em all how to do it. It's sickening."

"Man, don't go getting all melodramatic on me. I ain't down here for a course on the eternal plight of the haves

versus the have-nots. I need that bread bad so I can go back
to the States and clear some serious debt that's hanging
over my head. So the sooner we find and link up with your
buddy, this Vic Gabriel, the quicker we can get on with
what it is we're supposed to be doin'. You been down here
before with your buddy," Simms went on, looking around
the terminal in all directions, as if expecting someone to run
up to them and shoot them, or a parade of soldiers to
swarm over them and whisk them away to the nearest jail,
"so I'm trusting you to know how to handle things. Me, you
know I done three tours of duty in Nam, so if things get hot
in the bush, I'll be right there. Still, I ain't lookin' to get my
ass shot up, but I'll pull my weight, y'know that. Let's just
do whatever it is we gotta do and get back home in one
piece."

Dillinger grunted. Sure, okay, maybe Simms was right,
he thought. Skip the history lesson about the screwed-up mess
that was Central America. How can you make reason out of
insanity anyway? How do you explain the greed and desperation and appalling poverty that consumed Central America
and fed on itself until the whole damn thing had become a
monster nobody seemed capable of slaying? No, they weren't
there to change the world, and whatever it was they were
going to do wouldn't really have much bearing on the course
of events in Central America anyway. That didn't mean he
couldn't look around and call it like he saw it, Dillinger
thought. Still, they'd been paid to do a job and they would do
it. Exactly what his longtime friend Vic Gabriel had in mind,
Dillinger wasn't sure. Dillinger had been there in the jungles
of Nicaragua six months ago with Gabriel and stayed on for
two months, training Contra rebels under so-called CIA
supervision, and leading raiding parties against Sandinista
strongholds. Vic had opted to stay because he had claimed he
didn't have anything better to do. Dillinger didn't buy that.
He suspected there was more going on in Nicaragua with
Gabriel than his friend was willing to let on.

As he looked up the terminal, Dillinger froze in his
tracks. The guy stood out, head and shoulders above the
mob scene. It was a face, a face unlike any Dillinger had
ever seen and he thought he must be dreaming a bad

dream. A face he couldn't miss in a crowd. A face he wouldn't soon forget. It was as if he was staring at the face of Death itself and had been turned to stone by those cold piercing eyes. The man had CIA written all over him. The man looked as if he had held hands with Death for centuries. Dillinger had the unnerving sensation that he had just looked into the next world through the eyes in that death's-head. And it was a scary place that awaited.

Simms stopped when he realized Dillinger wasn't beside him. Turning, Simms called back, "What's with you now? Man, you're acting weird. Get your shit together, Bad One, or I hop on the next Aeronica bucket of bolts and head back for Miami."

Someone nudged Dillinger, distracted him for a moment, and he glowered at the Latino who bumped into him, the man then apologizing to him in rapid-fire Spanish. When Dillinger looked back up the terminal, the face was gone. Disappeared, as if the guy had never even been there. A chill walked down Dillinger's spine.

"Did you see him? Did you see that?"

Simms looked around. "See who? See what, man?"

"Forget it," Dillinger growled.

"Hey. You two."

The voice shot through the babble of Spanish like the crack of a pistol. Unnerved suddenly by the whole scene in the terminal, and like Simms, sensing something was wrong with the whole trip, Dillinger wheeled. The guy strode up to them in olive drab khakis and a sweat-stained white shirt, looking like any gringo tourist in the lower Americas, but Dillinger knew they'd found their contact. The man did everything but wear CIA emblazoned on his shirt.

"I'm Major Hawkins. Gabriel sent me to meet you."

No handshakes. No introductions. Dillinger and Simms gave the major a hard once-over. There was that steel in the major's voice that warned Dillinger he was all business, the business of war and death. Hawkins had a crew cut, a chiseled, square-jawed face, his eyes hidden by dark aviator shades.

"Where's Gabriel?" Dillinger asked. "He was supposed to meet us here."

"There's been a little problem. C'mon. I'll explain once we're outside Managua."

Dillinger exchanged grim looks with Simms.

Hawkins was already moving up the terminal. He looked back, waiting, scowling.

"This ain't working out already, Bad One. I don't like this at all. Somethin' smells."

"Hey, you two comin' or what? This isn't any sight-seeing tour I'm giving you. Shake a leg."

Dillinger and Simms followed their contact.

Major Hawkins had a jeep waiting for them outside the airport. Dillinger and Simms were told not to ask any questions, so they rode in silence until they were outside of Managua, heading northwest. Hawkins drove, with Dillinger in the passenger seat and Simms sitting in the back. Miles passed in hard silence as the major steered the jeep down jungle trails buzzing with insect noise and the screech of monkeys. There was no sign of human life anywhere for long stretches of dirt road. Warning bells kept wanting to go off in Dillinger's head. He was surprised at the ease with which they were allowed to pass three military roadblocks, unmolested by Sandinista soldiers. Dillinger asked Hawkins about this because all the major had to do was flash some kind of ID to the soldiers and they were free to go on their way.

"It's all fucked up down here right now in the aftermath of the big revolution," Hawkins said. "If you want to know the truth, the Company's got its fingers in both pies. You can't tell the players without a scorecard down here most of the time. I've paid off the comandante of the zone so that we're allowed free mobility—as long as we stick close to the Honduran border. That's where I'm taking you. Your buddy Gabriel, he's been shot up pretty bad and he's holed up at a border town. He was running a unit back and forth across the border, hitting some Sandinista strong points with his Contra rebels. His luck almost ran out. Took a couple of slugs in the upper chest, so he's been recuperating. That's why he didn't meet you at the airport. He's laid up and he's not in the best of shape. But I tell ya, your buddy Gabriel, he seems to have more than nine lives, but he might've used 'em all up. Needless to say, by his not dying, he's pissed off a lot of people down here."

Vic shot? Dillinger thought, worried. Laid up? Out of action maybe. This mysterious Major Hawkins, showing up unexpectedly out of nowhere, with all kinds of evasive answers to legitimate questions. The whole thing, like Simms kept saying, he thought, smelled. Smelled like death. Smelled like some kind of setup. Vic was in some kind of trouble, Dillinger was certain. But what was going down? And how badly was Vic really hurt? There was no doubt in Dillinger's mind that Gabriel would pull through all right. There are men like that, Dillinger knew, and liked to count himself among their ranks. They are faced with death, day in and day out, yet they always seem to beat the odds and survive. It's as if they have some kind of invincible aura around them and are protected by the fickle gods of fate and universal justice. Sure, they get scratched up, scarred up, and beaten down, but they keep coming back, tougher than ever. Vic Gabriel seemed to have more guardian angels watching over him than he could count, Dillinger thought, and had personally experienced the guy's blessing of fate rub off on him more than once. You are the comrades you keep, he decided, and there is safety in the womb of good and right because justice does win out eventually. It is faith you must keep that all will work out. When you stop believing, when you quit in despair, that is when it all comes crumbling down around you in ruins. It was a shame, Dillinger thought, that often he didn't have more faith. It was good that there were men around like Vic to kick him square in the ass when he needed it.

"I'm still not getting the picture here, Major," Dillinger said, and torched up a stogie with his Zippo. "Here's a country embroiled in war, crawling with Contras, Sandinistas, KGB and CIA, but yet you tell me a simple bribe allows us free rein to go wherever the hell it is we want to go, even when the other side knows what you're all about? Doesn't make any sense, Major. Try again. Let's tighten this act up some."

Hawkins was silent for several moments, then said, "All right. It's like this. The Company's got some rogues *down here, running guns, running dope, in short, kicking up a whole lot of shit you don't read about in the papers up north. Money buys favors down here. Greed and desperation rule down here. You play, you pay. You don't play, you pay. Apparently the CIA has been running in C130s chockful of weapons for the Contras, then those same planes are heading out loaded down with dope. Dope is big bucks, buys guns for the Contras so that the CIA can keep their little clandestine war going down here and save the Western Hemisphere from the evils of communism, or so goes the reasoning. Your buddy, Gabriel, not only does he not want to pay the other side or play ball with the more seedier elements so that all of us can get along, he seems to be down here on some personal crusade, and rumor has it he's looking for the killer of his father, one Michael Saunders. Ever hear of him?"*

"Yeah, I've heard of him. But Vic wouldn't call us down here, pay us good money up front just to reel us in to help him on some personal vendetta."

"Maybe he just needs the extra guns, who knows? You see, he and his rebels, they're stuck in this border town and the CIA doesn't seem capable or willing to help him get out. Y'know, for fear of stirring the pot and having wind of this getting back to Washington."

"So they'd just as soon see the man die," Johnny Simms growled, shaking his head in disbelief.

"What can I tell ya?" Hawkins said. *"It's all image, it all comes down to money. If word got out about what's really going on down here, it would be all over for a lot of people, important people. The* Washington Post *would have a field day.* MERCS IN NICARAGUA FOMENTING WAR, RUNNING GUNS AND DRUGS TO SAVE THE FREE WORLD FROM COMMUNISM. *That kinda thing. All aid to the Contras would get cut off quick as you can spit."*

"I'm still confused," Dillinger growled.

"So am I. The whole damn thing's confusing. It's like this, so you'd better find your balls and wear 'em. A major strike is being planned by both the Sandinistas and Salvadoran guerrillas and it's due to hit the border town some time in the next two days. They want to wipe out Gabriel

and his rebels because he's got a lock on that stretch of border. That's all I can really tell you."

"So we came down here just in time for the shelling to begin. Shit," Simms rasped.

"Something like that, soldier. Don't worry. You won't be alone when the shit starts flying."

"I can't tell ya how happy I am to hear that," Simms growled.

The major guided the jeep out of the jungle, through a series of high green hills, and Dillinger saw the border town. The first thing he noticed was the stench of death. The place looked like something out of the old American Wild West. Frontier town, with a main dirt street, rolling in stretches, dividing some adobe buildings and corrugated tin structures. Burros and horses and mongrels roamed the street, which was gutted with holes from recent shelling. Graffiti bearing anti-American slogans was scrawled across a number of the buildings. The jungle brushed right up against the town, and escaping the noises of animal and insect life was impossible. Dillinger saw Nicaraguans, all of them unarmed, lounging in the shadows of buildings, casting them hostile and suspicious looks. Where were all these Contra rebels? Where was all the hardware? he wondered, and felt the hackles begin to rise on the back of his neck. The trip to the border town had taken up the better part of the day, and Dillinger was suddenly feeling as if some dark mystery was waiting in the wings. Something brutal and violent and final. The sun was sinking beyond the distant hills, and long shadows were stretching over the border town. The heavy silence, the stink of death lent the whole damn place a haunting feel of suffering and decay.

"What about weapons?" Dillinger inquired.

The major stopped the jeep in front of a tin shack. "In there. With Gabriel. I guess you'll want a little time with him alone?"

Dillinger and Simms hopped out of the jeep, duffel bags in hand. Before Dillinger could reply, Hawkins said, "I'll be back. I got some things to take care of." And the jeep pulled away, forging down a jungle trail. Dillinger looked at Simms, who said, "Like I been saying, Bad One. Somethin' smells."

Inside the shack, Dillinger spotted a motionless lump in the far corner, stretched out on a pile of blankets. The smell of rot pierced his senses. A kerosene lamp hung from the ceiling, and as light flickered over the figure, which was bandaged around the shoulders and chest, Dillinger recognized Gabriel.

"Vic? Vic?"

A groan, and Gabriel stirred. Surprise hardened Gabriel's heavily bristled features. Vic looked gaunt, frail almost, to Dillinger. Then Gabriel looked shocked to see Dillinger.

"Dillinger? What the hell are you doing here? Who's that with you?"

Ice shivered down Dillinger's spine. "Wh-what . . . what the hell do you mean what am I doing here? You sent for me. What, have you got a fever and it's affected your memory, old man?"

Gabriel struggled to sit up. For several moments he just looked at Dillinger and Simms, confused.

"Major Hawkins," Dillinger said. "He picked us up at the airport. You know the major, don't ya? Told us you were waiting here for us. He drove us here."

"Hawkins? I don't know any Major Hawkins. I never sent for you."

Cold fear began to gnaw at Dillinger's guts. He looked at Johnny Simms, who groaned, a sound that seemed to echo the mounting anxiety Dillinger felt in that hovel, in this place of death and suffering.

Chapter 6

The more you look, the smaller your world becomes. The more you see, the heavier your heart can get. The more you feel, the less you really want to know.

They made it the six klicks to San Pedro without further incident. Vic Gabriel, his commandos, and *El Tigre* led the Contra fighting force into the squalor of the refugee camp. A hellhole, Gabriel saw, swarming with human suffering, a place alive with death. He couldn't help but hear his father's voice in his head. *The more you look . . . the more you see . . . the more you feel . . .* Over and over, again and again. He had seen poverty and intense human suffering before in many parts of the world, but it never failed to affect him. No matter where he saw it, his heart always grew heavy. Suddenly his own problems seemed small in comparison, remote and trivial. Strip away his ideals and belief in the sanctity of human life, and he, like Simms, Boolewarke, and Dillinger, was just a soldier of fortune. Vic Gabriel had long since accepted his life, and he knew the degree of suffering and danger that went with it. Some choose the cross they carry, others have it thrust upon their shoulders. Not a bleeding heart by any means, Vic Gabriel knew that, sadly, most of the world lives in poverty and ignorance through mostly no fault of their own. That's just the way it is. Knowing that didn't make him feel any less compassion for the tortured souls who were swept up in a war other men created. While the few fat cats played their big game, the rest slowly die, or are forgotten, or are ignored. That's just the way it is. The Big Table in life is set for only the lucky few. You are dealt a certain card when you come into the world, he thought, and in every deck there are only so many aces to go around. It is fortunate, after all, that nothing lasts for long. In the scope of eternity each life passes through the light in the blink of an eye, and they make of it all what they will. There is death, and then there is justice, and in that mystery alone all riddles are solved. He had often heard that there is no justice in the world. There isn't. Justice comes later. And then the Big Table is empty. All the kings are dead, and only the worms feed on. Mouths that devoured, eyes that were blind, hearts that didn't care or grew cold to it all, tongues that spoke in lies and denial and vanity . . . there will be answers to the riddle, and there will be no escaping it. If there isn't any justice at the end of the eyeblink, he thought, then none of this means a damn thing and the biggest joke of all has been played on the human race for even being here in the first place. If that is the case, then men are free to blind themselves to it all, to devour, to lie, to live as if there is no tomorrow because tomorrow doesn't mean a thing. Only the voice in your head, your conscience, keeps the fine line drawn between the bonded criminality of the human race. Only the sociopath, the psychopath, or the truly evil don't hear it, and they are the ones who make us wonder if any of this is really all worth it, and if any of this really means a damn thing. Perhaps, they are the freest ones of all, although they, too, cannot escape the eyeblink factor.

What Vic Gabriel now saw was that bonded criminality overshadowing and overpowering those who would never sit at the Big Table.

Low-lying adobe structures, pockmarked and scarred by bullets and mortar barrages that had long ago hit the village and left behind more dead, dying, and mutilated victims of the Nicaraguan civil war. Everywhere, Gabriel saw the signs of violent conflict, and his heart felt like some great sagging weight in his chest. There were children with missing arms and legs. Women, who had once been young and pretty and vital, now old and haggard and defeated at thirty or forty. Squads of *El Tigre*'s men, who had been left behind to guard the village, haunted and disillusioned, many of them bandaged and maimed, blind or missing a limb. Graffiti, some of it denouncing the current regime, some of it denouncing the CIA, scrawled across the facades of gutted buildings. Small fires cooking meat, and mongrel dogs scavenging the fly-and-mosquito-ravaged scraps that were probably even unfit for human consumption. There really were no good guys down here, Gabriel thought, only the dead and the dying, so don't believe all the bullshit you read in the newspapers back home, son, because most of those people are fighting each other to get to the Big Table and they'll take the scraps if that's all they can get. Only suffering and misery and dying was alive and well in Nicaragua. These people weren't even living day-to-day. It was a second-to-minute existence, where they waited for the next rocket attack, or for a Sandinista patrol to come storming through the village, or for the few scraps of food to run out, or disease to set in and slowly suck the life right out of the soul. The second hand on the Great Clock was always ticking toward the grinning death's-head, faster and faster, and it waited for no man, and certainly spared no one. There was an atmosphere of fear that Gabriel felt hanging over the village, a heavy, oppressive weight. And a stink of decay. A smell of death and dying things. Land reforms? What's that? Just another dictator doing business as usual in Central America, claiming to be for the little man, but grabbing everything he can for himself in the name of freedom. Free elections? No such thing. It was a front, a veneer to keep Uncle Sam happy and spewing forth more aid into the lower Americas. Haven't you heard? They're making room for you at the Big Table, son. So roll up, eat well, be flashy, live good. You can't do anything about the plight of the little man anyway, right? So why worry about it? Take what you can, get your fill, because it might all be gone tomorrow.

"Things sure haven't changed much since we were last here," Johnny Simms commented, looking around, shaking his head. "Same old shit. Man, and I thought I used to have it bad when I was a kid running the streets. Not even the worst part of D.C. can compare to this."

"Same old bullshit, yeah, Johnny boy, except more

people are dying," Dillinger said, "and somebody sitting over all this misery is getting rich. Living the good life. Doesn't make a damn bit of sense. Not a goddamn bit of sense."

Gabriel fired up a Marlboro with a flick of his Zippo. "*El Tigre*, we need to talk about tonight."

"My God, it's true! The four *mercenarios*. It's true! My God, I can't tell you gentlemen how good it is to see you! Americans! American faces! American fighting men. Fighting for the cause of freedom! Fighting the oppressive Sandinista regime! My God, you're like a vision!"

They stopped cold in their tracks. Gabriel spotted the long-haired, bearded guy with about three thousand dollars' worth of camera equipment draped from his camos running toward them. He wore gold around his neck and jewelry around his fingers—not a very smart thing to do in a place where starving people would cut your throat for a bowl of rice and beans. The grin split the guy's beard, and Gabriel saw a shark in man's clothing. It is not hard to pick them out. They are small carnivorous creatures, circling the outer fringes of human misery, sniping and chomping off pieces of the host body to keep themselves fat and happy. They come in many forms, many shapes, are seen in many places. The big suits in the big corporations who can destroy the environment and shrug it off while they chase a buck. The used-car salesman hustling a grotesquely over-priced deathtrap to somebody's grandmother. The whore on the streets selling death between her legs while she wears the pasted-on smile on painted lips, as she breathes lies and deceit that stink of the grave, as she lures you to your end, steals your balls and your soul, a black-widow spider claiming to have a heart of gold. The big-time prizefighter's manager-promoter, raking in millions for signing a piece of paper and all the while claiming he's worth that bundle while his fighter is out there risking getting his brains punched out through his ears. They lie, they cheat, they bullshit. This is their real, their only talent, mainly because they are lazy and hunger for the good life, never finding themselves or their real honest talents because they never bothered to look. It is simply too much trouble, requires more energy than they are willing to expend to make an honest go at it. They can often be excused but rarely ignored, because it is you who can become their next victim.

In this case, it was the yellow photojournalist, out to make a name for himself. He would get his story, and go back to the States and sell it, then thump his chest at happy hour and impress all the women and buy drinks for everybody willing to endure him. It is style without substance, and you become a body without heart or soul. It is a form of slow death without realizing that you are dying.

Zac Dillinger nearly snapped his stogie in two with his mouth as he looked at the guy and growled, "What the fuck is that? What is that thing supposed to be?"

Disdain etched *El Tigre*'s face. "That, hombres, is the Hippie. A free-lance photojournalist and scribbler. An insect we do not seem to be able to get rid of."

"The Hippie?" Dutch rasped.

"You ever try a good spray of Raid?" Dillinger added.

"My God, let me get some pictures. . . ."

Hippie began snapping away with his camera, sidling in front of Eagle Force like some carnivorous spider. He was grinning from ear to ear, and the only thing he didn't do, Gabriel thought, was cry, "Say cheese."

Gabriel had seen enough of the Hippie. "Dutch!"

"My pleasure, old man."

The ex–Recces commando snatched the camera out of Hippie's hands and snapped it off his scrawny neck. Before Hippie could protest, Dutch stomped the camera into the dirt.

"Why did you do that?" Hippie cried. "I just wanted a few pictures. Jesus Christ! That's five hundred dollars' worth of camera you smashed up!"

"I know," Dutch cracked, "I'm just a big brute who has no culture but who sure as hell knows exploitation when he sees it. Beat it, dog meat! Before I kick you in the nuts."

As Gabriel brushed past Hippie, he said, "We're not down here looking for our story to make the silver screen, jack. The Four *Mercenarios* aren't exactly the Four Musketeers."

"Best you stay out of our faces, man," Simms warned Hippie, and rolled up beside the other commandos.

Hippie looked at the crushed ruins of his camera, seemed on the verge of tears. "Unbelievable. Unbelievable, man. How am I supposed to make a living with all this hostility surrounding me? No one understands. No one understands poetry anymore, man, no one. It doesn't make any sense. No poetry, just all this hostility."

El Tigre was smiling. "I do like your style, Comandante Gringo. That one, he is a nuisance, but, perhaps, who knows, whatever he writes, it may make an impression back in the States and, who knows, aid our cause."

"The only thing that one will be aiding," Bad Zac growled, "is his wallet. All we need is some clown like that getting our ugly mugs printed up in the *Washington Post* and we're as compromised as a whore's crotch. Every law-enforcement agency and intelligence network in the world would have our heads mounted as trophies. We've been down some roads we'd rather not have too many people knowing about, if you catch my drift."

El Tigre was nodding, still smiling, but the smile had turned grim. "*Sí*. I understand. Believe me, your true identities will never be compromised because of me."

As the wounded were carried toward the ruins of the village church, the four *mercenarios* walked slowly down the middle of the main dirt street, and they became the focus of undivided and intense scrutiny. Gabriel felt the dark stares boring into his back like drills. Eyes sought them out from deep inside the shadows of rubble. Emaciated frames holding weapons stood in the gloomy recesses of open tin huts, watching them with wary stares, like they would some predatory jaguar. The sick and the wounded, lying beneath cardboard or filthy blankets, peered out from a private world of misery. A dog trotted in front of the four mercenaries, sniffing at them, then scampering away, too tired or weak to bark at strangers. They were like some aliens, and they were from another world, after all. They were invaders from a distant land, another time. No, Gabriel didn't expect them to be welcomed with open arms, a horde of well-wishers showering them with roses, women rushing up to them and hugging and kissing them, the conquering heroes, the freers of the oppressed. It didn't work that way, but it rarely does. They were what they were, and everyone there in San Pedro knew what they were, even if they didn't know what they were about.

"They may appear hostile, hombres," *El Tigre* informed Eagle Force, "but they aren't. Word has long since reached San Pedro from my men. You will be treated with respect. You are with me. And they know that you did not come here empty-handed, that you are here to help."

Gabriel checked the surrounding jungle, then looked up at the cobalt sky. A flock of vultures circled San Pedro, swimming slowly and gracefully in the shimmering heat thermals. Flies picked at his sweaty, stubbled face.

The ex–Special Forces warrior returned his gaze to the street.

And he saw her.

A young, half-naked urchin nearly walked up Gabriel's back as the tall commander of Eagle Force stopped cold in his tracks. Anxiety on his filthy face, the boy peered around Gabriel's leg.

Lolita stood there in the middle of the street, her M16 slung around her shoulder. She didn't budge, just stared at Gabriel. There was defiance in the way she stood.

The three commandos looked from the lone beautiful woman to their leader. Gabriel felt frozen in time, felt his mouth trying to open, but words were locked in his chest. He couldn't believe his eyes. He felt ice, then fire, then ice again. He felt rooted to the spot, the breath trapped in his throat. And it had been just like this, the first time he'd ever seen her. Years ago. When he had first laid eyes on her, the most beautiful woman he'd ever seen anywhere in the world.

Gabriel felt a hand tugging at his pants leg. He looked down, saw the dirty boyish face cut in a wide grin.

"Lolita, she's very pretty, eh, señor?"

Gabriel returned his stare to the lone woman. "Very pretty, son, very pretty, yeah."

"I take it you know the señorita, old man?" Henry van Boolewarke said.

Gaze fixed on Lolita, Gabriel told his troops, "Stay here. Or do something to stay busy. I'll be back in a while."

Slowly, Gabriel moved away from his troops, feeling as if he'd stepped back in time. A hundred questions poured through his head. A dozen feelings threatened to overpower him.

Simms and Dillinger looked at each other, and Dutch caught the glint in their eyes. "Let's give the old man some time to himself, and I suggest you two whoredogs watch the wisecracks. This looks serious from where I stand."

"Who is she?" Dillinger asked *El Tigre*.

"She is Lolita Armandez. She belongs to no man. She is her own woman. Very tough. Very strong. Very beautiful. Very deadly, too. She is one of the best fighters under my command."

Simms looked respectful as he said, "'Nuf said."

Gabriel came to within a foot of her, and stared deep into her eyes. He felt mesmerized by her, locked in his own private memories of what they had shared so long ago. She was still beautiful, even though there was a hard look in her eyes, a quiet suffering about her, which wasn't difficult for Gabriel to understand. She just stared back at him, and he couldn't read her expression. She still radiated a quiet savage intensity that had intrigued him so long ago.

"Lolita." It was all he could say.

Her eyes softened. "It is true what I heard. You are alive and you have come back. For what? The war? To fight? To make big dinero off the war?"

"I . . . I . . ."

"You are what, Gabriel? Sorry? Sorry that you left me? Without a word? Without any explanation?"

He tried a smile, but it felt foolish as he said, "You gonna shoot me?"

She returned the smile, with a hint of sorrow in the dark pools of her eyes. "I should. *Sí.* Where it would hurt you most."

He felt the eyes of his troops, the eyes of all the villages boring into him like a drill. "Can we talk somewhere?"

The smile was almost contemptuous. "Talk? Or what? Perhaps the fire still burns?"

"Perhaps."

"I will not pretend to stand here and melt like some silly schoolgirl."

"I don't expect you to."

"Follow me. We will talk."

But the fire still burned, and the talking waited until after the flames cooled. The flames cooled some, but the fire, Vic Gabriel could tell, would never die. Even though so much had happened since the last time they'd seen each other, their feelings for each other, that burning hunger that went deeper than just wanting to know each other physically, a feeling that burned right to the core of their beings and made them want to know each other's souls, was still there. Always had been. Always would be. Perhaps, Vic Gabriel thought, after all is said and done and a man achieves in life what he sets out to do, the only thing that really matters is one man, one woman, and how they feel about each other. Time, distance, trauma, tragic events can separate two people from each other, but what was there, if it was real to begin with, will always remain. Once in a great while, in a rare moment of stability that bordered on insanity and self-loathing, Vic Gabriel wondered if his life could have been, or still could be, different somehow. He always ended up telling himself things were what he had made them. It is best not to live with regrets, to deal with the moment, and learn from your mistakes.

Vic Gabriel stood, soaked in the sweat of their passion, and dressed. He lit a Marlboro and looked at Lolita. She was stretched out on soiled blankets, her long lean figure covered by an equally soiled blanket. Flies and mosquitoes buzzed through the hut.

Gabriel looked long and hard into those deep dark pools, captivated by the incredible beauty of this woman, mesmerized by her quiet savage intensity. The smell of her sweat, her musk made him want to take her again. He felt foolish. He didn't know what to say. He knew how it had ended, so many years ago. At a time when he was torn up

over the death of his father, he had also received word that
his brother, his only living relative, was in trouble with
drugs and heavily in debt to drug dealers. How could he
possibly make her understand that without it sounding like
so much bullshit rationale and justification? The fire in their
lovemaking was still there. They still hungered for each
other, just as it had been, years ago. So much had
happened, but it was still there between them. Would she
then listen, he thought, to his excuses and bullshit? Was he
looking for her forgiveness? Was he looking to unload his
own burden of guilt? Could they be lovers again? Maybe
somehow make it different? Make it last? Dammit, just
what the hell was he thinking anyway? He had three other
men with him, and they were committed to the ideals and
to the war of Eagle Force. Was there a place for her?

"You're still the most beautiful woman I've ever
known, Lolita. The fire still burns. At least for me."

She grunted, her gaze torn between sorrow and anger.
"Unfortunately, flattery will get you everywhere. Why?
Why?" she suddenly asked, and sat up, wrapping the
blanket around her. "Tell me, why?"

He knew what she was asking. There were no answers.
At least none that he thought she would accept.

"I don't know, Lolita, I don't know. I can't stand here
and say I'm sorry, even though I am. A lot was going on in
my life. Many things. Terrible things. How do you justify
the insanity of life? How can anybody make sense of what
goes on in the world? I didn't want to burden you."

"What? You think because I am a woman I wouldn't
understand these terrible things you allude to after living
my life in Nicaragua? What? What were these other things
you never even told me about? You never even told me
why you just had to leave. No explanations. No apologies.
It was like we never existed. Surely, we were more to each
other than that."

"We were, we were. I hope . . . I hope perhaps we
still are . . . or can be. All right, I'll tell you why I
left . . . at least in my own mind why I felt I had to leave
so suddenly. My father had recently been murdered. I was
devastated. I was looking for the man responsible for his

murder, and that's how I ended up in Nicaragua to begin with. What were you, eighteen, nineteen when I first saw you?"

She nodded. "Old enough to carry a weapon and fight the Sandinistas by your side."

A weak smile danced over Gabriel's lips. "I remember. It was beautiful, Lolita, the whole experience. Going into the jungle together, risking our lives, side by side, then having each other to love and comfort every night. I often have wished it could have lasted forever. I've thought about you often . . . and missed you. The reason I left . . . I got word that my brother was in trouble back in the States. I had to go to him, go find him."

"What kind of trouble?"

"Drug trouble. It killed him. I found him dead. Instead of finding him and trying to save him in time . . . he was dead. Just like my father. Dead. The insanity of life killed them both, but in slightly different ways."

"And you never bothered to come back and find me and tell me this?"

"I loved you, Lolita, like no other woman I've ever known."

"*Sí.* I believe you, or I would not have given myself to you again like this. We were always so passionate together. Our love was like a fire, that just kept growing and growing, burning and burning. But like a wildfire, did our love grow out of control? Did you become afraid?"

"Of what?"

"Of us," she answered. "That you would become tied to me. I understand men like you, Gabriel. There is very little place in your life for a woman. Believe me, the love we shared, I would have waited, I would have done anything you wanted me too. I would have been happy, content to wait for you while you went off and did whatever it was you had to do. Did you not think I would understand?"

Gabriel took a deep drag on his smoke. He walked over to her, knelt down, and cupped her face with a hand. She was so beautiful, he thought, so understanding, so passionate, so full of life even in a place teeming with death and misery. Even after all this time, she was still so alive in a way that very few are. And how she must have hated him bitterly for just up and leaving her. She was right in that she deserved to know why.

"You deserve more than that, Lolita. You deserve more than me just going off and fighting my own wars and then coming back to you. Not knowing when I'd be leaving again, or why, or if I'll ever come back."

Renewed anger sparked her eyes. "I deserve more than this, too!" she growled, glaring around at the hovel. "What I deserved was a father for our son."

Gabriel felt his heart skip a beat. "Wh-what?"

"That's right." Tears welled in her eyes. "A son. The son you left me with when you went off . . . to fight your own war in the States."

He stared at her, felt his lips moving, but was unable to find any words. It was like he'd been suddenly cast into a dream and was trying to wake up.

"It's true. I would not make something like this up. There are others who can tell you. It is true."

"A son . . . where . . ."

"He's dead."

A flurry of emotions swept through Vic Gabriel. Disbelief. Confusion. Sorrow. Anger. He knew she was not the type of woman to lie about something so serious, to make him feel guilty. There was stone-cold conviction in her eyes and in her voice.

"Dead," she told him, and her voice cracked. "His name was Juan. Juan Gabriel I called him," she said, and a thin smile stretched her lips as she looked down, a tear breaking from the corner of her eye. "There were things in him . . . I saw you in him. Like us, I guess it wasn't meant to last. The war, it killed him. They killed him. The Sandinistas."

As the tears broke from her eyes, Gabriel flicked his smoke aside and held her. Silently, he let her weep, and he, too, felt like crying for the son he'd never known.

She looked up, and fire burned beneath the tears in her eyes. "Listen to me, I go with you. Whatever you are doing here, I do not care. I go with you. I fight with you. When it is time for you to go . . . I will understand."

It was like acid was eating away behind his eyeballs. He clenched his jaw, moved by her passion, her feeling for him and the son she had lost. Her love was without question, without regret or bitterness. Yeah, he thought, she deserved so much more. A woman like her was rare in any country, in any part of the world. She had heart. She had guts.

Gabriel nodded.. "All right."

"Then love me again," Lolita Armandez said, and pulled Vic Gabriel down on top of her. "Love me like there will be no tomorrow. Love me. God, I love you. A part of me hates you for loving you so much."

And they let the fire burn. Out of control. For perhaps the last time.

He knew she was right.

Tomorrow might never come.

Chapter 7

The Hippie was starting to drive Henry van Boolewarke to the edge of a murderous rage. But the Dutchman was concerned more about his friend, Vic Gabriel, and the present status of Eagle Force inside Nicaragua. So the ex–Recces commando sat among the rubble inside the church with Simms and Dillinger beside him, and spooned cold rice and beans into his mouth, sipped tepid water from his canteen, and tuned the Hippie out.

A woman. Worse, Dutch thought, a woman that Vic had obviously been seriously involved with before when he had been there in Nicaragua, years ago when Vic had been a paramilitary operative for the CIA. The Dutchman had seen the look in their eyes for each other, felt the heat of passion between them. Damn. A woman. And a beautiful, fiery woman with a powerful presence at that. A woman like that could grab a man by the balls and squeeze and all the while he thinks it feels good. A woman like that could be the worst possible distraction for a soldier and cause him ultimately to get himself and others killed on the battle-field. Not that he had anything against women, no. Dutch had known and loved more than a few beautiful women himself, loved them intensely, passionately, as only a man who knows tomorrow may never come can. All kinds of women. He'd loved them all, and if Dillinger or Simms thought they were lady-killers, he thought, well, they hadn't seen him in action yet. A woman can be a good thing for a man, especially a soldier, because she can give him a place in her heart for comfort and warmth and understanding, allow him to escape, temporarily, the harsh realities of his existence of living and ultimately knowing he has to die by the sword. But there's a time and a place for everything. When a man is as driven, can be as single-minded in pursuing an objective as Vic Gabriel, a woman can be a lethal distraction, no if's, and's, or but's about it.

Right now their situation was grave. They were a couple of hundred klicks deep inside the Nicaraguan jungle, surrounded by Sandinistas looking to dislodge them from the zone with massive firepower. They were supposed to raid the garrison of Attila the Hun and free an American colonel who had most likely been sent there on orders by the CIA. The small army of *El Tigre* had just been made smaller by the ambush, as Dutch heard the feeble groans of wounded men drift to him from deep inside the shadows of the church rubble. Nuns and a big priest in black habit hustling to administer to the wounded kept casting hostile glances toward the *mercenarios*. San Pedro, like many African villages Dutch had seen during bush wars in Angola and Mozambique, stank of death and despair and misery. All of them were trapped in hell.

And the Hippie just babbled on.

All four of them, Dutch thought, were right there, right there at the edge, walking the edge of the blade, dancing with a devil laughing in their faces. One wrong move, one slip, and that edge would slice them up until there was nothing left for even the buzzards to feed on.

"Man, this is the classic struggle between the oppressed and the oppressor. Can't you see it? The classic struggle between the haves and the have-nots. Check it out, man, this is just one example. *MISURASATA*. Ever hear of it?"

Johnny Simms finished his beans and rice and looked at the Hippie, who was squatting in the dirt in front of the three mercs, puffing anxiously on a cigarette.

"It's an acronym for the Miskito, Suma, Rama, Asla, and Takanka Indians," Simms answered. "I think I know what you're driving at, Hippie Man. You're gonna tell me that in the name of this classic struggle between the haves and have-nots the Sandinistas have relocated all these Indian peoples, driven them off their land. . . ."

"Yeah, yeah, you got some of the big picture, brother," Hippie said, and caught a baleful glower from Simms. "The Sandinistas, man, the Great Oppressors, they burn the crops and villages of the Indians and put them in concentration camps. They steal the best farmland from the Indians and use it for themselves, just like they take it from the campesinos. That's just one example of typical Sandinista piggery and oppression. Man, there are a hundred thousand new mouths to feed in this country every year. One of the highest growth rates and also one of the highest illiteracy rates in Latin America, and one of the most oppressive, lying, cheating, murdering dictatorial regimes in Latin American history, the Sandinistas, lording over the whole mess and trying to keep both the Great Uncle and Ivan from rocking the boat. Nicaragua is a time bomb surrounded by time bombs. The economy is shot, so how do the Sandinistas expect to live up to the promises of the revolution? They're going to export the revolution, man. Into Honduras. Into El Salvador. War is big business, man. War saves shattered economies. War takes care of the have-nots by getting rid of them so that the haves have more for themselves and less mouths to have to worry about feeding. We're looking at another Vietnam down here, man. And when the Great Uncle steps in, it's all gonna blow up in everybody's faces. The Indian, he's just in the way, and he will be trampled into the dust in the name of progress and the revolution. Much the same thing happened to the American Indian. Man, can't you see the connection? It's all there, the writing on the wall. Man is doomed, and I'll tell ya why. If man can't understand and remember history, he's doomed to repeat it. Things will probably never really get better down here, because the haves are too few and too powerful, and the have-nots too many and too weak. Only the great equalizer of death and destruction, man, keeps the entire fiasco from just feeding on itself and snowballing its way all the way into the States. Either way, man, we're talking about it feeding on itself anyway, and someday, man, someday the States will have to take notice because the whole world is going to be consumed in the classic revolution of the haves versus the have-nots. This is what the Russians are saying, man. A few just can't have it all while the rest are deprived of basic living. You can't horde all the good shit in life and expect not to piss somebody off."

Dutch looked the Hippie dead in the eye. "And where will you be when all this blowing up is going on, mate, when the big revolution goes down? Safe and secure somewhere back in the States, sitting on your big story, thumping your chest and telling everybody I told you so?"

Hippie shook his head. "Man, I was hoping you guys would be on my side. I'm a writer, a photojournalist, man, not a fighter, not a soldier. I'm a purveyor of truth, I carry the message and let others decide for themselves. I was hoping you were here to help crush the oppressors, to help me carry the message to the oppressed and ignorant masses."

"We're here on personal business, Long Hair," Bad Zac Dillinger growled. "We don't intend to be in this country any longer than necessary. Look, we're tired, and a little worried about our own asses, and speaking for myself, if I have to look at your scroungy ass much longer, I'm gonna get more than just a little bent out of shape. We're just some tired-ass dogs of war, so just get out of our faces and go write your great story about the classic world revolution that's coming. Let us be. Best advice I can give ya."

"As I suspected. You are common mercenaries. Common killers. Who do you work for? The CIA? Some big American corporation looking to cut a slice in Central America? Yourselves for personal gain?"

The commandos looked up, and Hippie swung his head sideways.

"Father Hercado," Hippie breathed, then told the commandos, "the village padre."

Father Hercado was a tall, dark-skinned, dark-haired priest whose eyes burned with conviction and the eternal anger of that conviction.

"Our country has suffered greatly since the Sandinistas came to power," Father Hercado told the commandos. "And it will continue to suffer, to have death and misery visited upon it as long as Nicaragua is being tugged about by the so-called superpowers. You men, you come, you take, you kill, you leave. And you leave in your wake more dead, more destruction, more misery. I am sick of being witness to all the death and misery this war has brought—"

"But you got God's calling to fulfill, right, padre?" Johnny Simms growled.

"Excuse me? You dare to be so irreverent against the word and works of God? What can I expect, though, from common soldiers of fortune?"

"No one's bein' anythin', padre," Simms answered, moderating his tone. "You, nor this long-haired scribbler here has got the first fucking idea of what the hell it is we're doing here. We're not here to upscale the war or make a bunch of money, or because of the CIA. We're here to rescue a friend of a friend. That's it. Bottom line. Not here for the money or the so-called glory of being a dog of war."

A mean smile cracked Bad Zac Dillinger's lips. He fired up a fat stogie. "Like Johnny boy says, padre, it's personal business and it ain't none of yours. 'Sides, with you spouting all this word of God all over us, how the hell we know that maybe you aren't the informant who brought that ambush down on us, huh?"

Father Hercado's lip quivered. "That's ridiculous!"

Dutch picked up the ball. "Is it, old man? Do tell. Best thing you can do, Father, is get that size-ten out of your mouth and go treat the wounded with the medicine and supplies we four heathens brought to San Pedro."

Father Hercado squared his shoulders. "Regardless of what you are, despite your blasphemy and disrespect for the Lord your God, I will pray for your souls. If I am wrong about you, then the Lord God shall be my judge, not you."

Father Hercado wheeled and left to tend to the wounded. The Hippie smirked.

"Man, that was great. You dudes don't take no shit from no one. I love it."

The three commandos leveled one collective dark stare on the Hippie, who held his hands up in resignation.

"Got you, dudes. All right. I'm splitting. But *El Tigre's* already said I can tag along on this march tonight, so don't get all worked up when you see me fall in with the troops."

Dillinger muttered a curse. "That's between you and the Tiger. But if you can't hold your own in a fight, don't come running to hide behind us."

"Fair enough, dude. Fair enough."

And the Hippie, grinning, stood and slid away from the commandos.

When the Hippie was out of earshot, Dutch told Simms and Dillinger, "I'm worried."

"About Vic?" Dillinger said.

"Right."

"Lolita?" Simms posed.

"Right. Complications. We don't need any more problems than we've already got. That woman, she could be trouble. Christ, how long's Victor been gone and shacked up with her?"

Dillinger checked his Rolex. "Three hours and twenty minutes. Must be having a helluva time. That's some R&R these old warbones could use, I'll tell ya that."

"The sun's setting," Simms said, "and we need to be getting this show on the road before there ain't no show at all. The Sandinistas could come storming through San Pedro anytime and blow our asses all the way back into Honduras."

"Problems?"

Their heads jerked sideways. A tall silent shadow, Vic Gabriel rolled out of the gloom and stood before his troops. There was a hard edge to his voice and a look in his eyes that warned Dutch he had overheard their conversation. Another shadow pulled up beside Vic Gabriel, materialized into the beautiful Lolita Armandez. An M16 was slung around her shoulder and there was a determined look in her eyes.

"We were just getting a little worried about you, Victor, that's all, old man," Dutch said, and his voice suddenly sounded small and weak to his ears.

"Don't be. Let's go find *El Tigre* . . . and, uh, get this show on the road before the sun sets."

Johnny Simms spoke up, appeared embarrassed.

"Look, Vic, we were just worried about you, that's all, man. Whatever else is going on, it's your business."

"Right. Remember that."

"Vic?"

Gabriel looked at Dutch. "What?"

Dutch looked at Lolita, cleared his throat. "Is she . . . is she, uh, going with us?"

"Yeah, she is. I hope nobody has a problem with that."

Gabriel and Lolita left the three commandos alone.

Dutch heaved a pent-up breath, his stare wandering between Simms and Dillinger.

Nobody said a word. Only the soft moaning of the wounded Contras shattered the hard silence between the commandos.

"Man, this is weird, this is weird. We been set up," Johnny Simms said. "I knew it, I knew it."

"Not by me, you haven't, so don't take it personal," Gabriel said.

Dillinger just stood in the flickering kerosene light, stunned and worried. "Vic, if you didn't send for us, then who did?"

Teeth gritted, Gabriel stood.

"Death. Death sent for you."

All heads turned. A middle-aged woman with long dark hair and a black dress and black hose stood in the doorway in the far corner. She looked straight ahead, her stare glazed, fixed on nothing, yet everything it seemed. Her eyes looked empty, lifeless.

"That's Inessa," Gabriel told the two men.

Simms stared at the woman. "Is she . . . she's . . ."

"Yeah. Blind since birth," Gabriel said. "She's considered the local prophet, fortune-teller—psychic, I guess you'd call her back home. She's no carnival sideshow. She's made a number of predictions over the years that have apparently come true. She also put me back together and broke my fever. I owe her. Do right by her, she'll hang with you."

"Man, this is weird, like I said, Bad One."

"Who's your buddy, Zac?"

"This is Johnny Simms. I can vouch for him. He's one of us."

Gabriel checked Simms out. The black man had the look that Gabriel had seen, time and again, in soldiers who had been out there in the killing fields, that hard, haunted look, the look of more than just being a survivor, the look of a warrior, committed to personal ideals and intent on destroying the enemy. And Gabriel sensed Simms was the kind of soldier who would go to bat for a fellow warrior, would stay entrenched and fight to his last breath. Gabriel held out his hand and both men shook. Gabriel had a good feeling about the man right away, and if Dillinger okayed Simms, Gabriel could go with that.

"Wish I could say 'welcome aboard,'" Gabriel told Simms. "But we've got trouble and I'm sorry you have to get involved. It's a helluva an introduction."

Simms wore a grim smile. "Tell me about it."

"The one who is Death, he sent a man to lure you here," Inessa said. "Death called you. Death waits."

"Death?" Dillinger growled. "Who's she talking about, VG? She's talking about Death like it's somebody we all know."

"Saunders. Michael Saunders."

"Death owns this country and He is coming for the three of you," Inessa went on. "I feared that my saving your life, Vic Gabriel, would be in vain."

"Vic, maybe you'd better explain and clue me and Johnny here in on what the hell's going on?"

"I didn't send for you, that I can tell you," Gabriel began. "Months before you were last here, the Company got me to work for them and organize their own Contra death squads to strike out against the Sandinistas. What I found, I found the Company, like the bastards did in Nam, are running guns and dope through Central America. There's a huge rogue operation down here, black-market stuff, and Saunders has got his hands deep in it. I didn't want to be here to begin with, but Saunders was what lured me here originally. You see, I cut a deal with the Company about a year ago. I launched my own war against the drug lords in the states, but the Company found out what I was *doing and was going to see I spent the rest of my life in prison unless I played ball with them. They said they wanted me to run the Contra operation in this zone, and they also said Saunders was down here and I could have him if I could find him and take him. Saunders murdered my father, but you already know that. I want the bastard— dead, by my own hand. Obviously he knows I'm here. They're coming for me, us. Tonight maybe."*

"Tonight, they are," Inessa said. "I feel the town. It is emptying around us, even as we speak."

Dillinger and Simms went to the door. Gabriel followed. Like Inessa said, Gabriel saw droves of men, women, and children walking off into the jungle with their few meager earthly possessions.

"Why us, Vic?" Dillinger asked. "I mean, if I can help you out, save your ass, I'm glad I'm here, but why did this Saunders bring us down here for an execution?"

Gabriel shrugged. "Not sure really, but I know the way the man thinks. You're the last connection I have to this world, and if he knows we're friends, it will make it that much tougher on me to have to watch him kill you . . . and now Simms."

"Not without a fight, he ain't," Simms growled. "What about weapons? You got weapons, don't ya?"

"In the back room. A little cache I got buried," Gabriel said. "An M60, and a couple of M16s with M203 launchers. Three dozen grenades. Some commando daggers. We'll be ready."

"Not if they send a few hundred guns into town," Simms said. "Oh, well, I guess there's worse places to die."

"What about your unit?" Dillinger asked. "I thought you had a small army of Contras under your command?"

"Wiped out. Two weeks ago. That's when I got shot up. Crawled back here, and Inessa, like I said, saved my life. What made you bring somebody along with you anyway?" Gabriel said, looking from Simms to Dillinger.

Inessa spoke up. "He is going to say 'because he had nothing better to do.'"

"How did you . . . how did she . . . forget it. Let's grab that hardware."

"*Inessa,*" *Gabriel said, leading Dillinger and Simms across the room, "you got a way out of here? Can you get safely out of this town and into the hills maybe?"*

"*I can hide in a safe place until the battle is over.*"

"*I wonder if she can tell us who's gonna win this battle?*" *Simms wondered aloud.*

"*Both sides will win. Both sides will lose. Death is always the loser. There will be plenty of death. I can feel it in the air.*"

"*That makes me feel a whole lot better,*" *Simms gruffed.*

Just then, the familiar whapping bleat of rotor blades rolled over the hut. The whirring of chopper blades hovered outside for several moments, the hovel shuddering in the rotor wash.

"*They're here. Showtime,*" *Gabriel said.*

The rotor wash vanished, and only hard silence and the stink of death filled the hut as the chopper moved away.

"*Where's this hardware, VG?*" *Dillinger growled. "Me and Johnny boy here, we might as well earn our keep.*"

SPETSNAZ Major Ivan Kubchkin was faced with some weighty decisions. He massaged his high-cheekboned, grizzled face, wiped the sweat out of the corner of his eye. Flies and mosquitoes buzzed through his tent, and he thought briefly of how much he hated the Nicaraguan jungle, or any jungle for that matter. He had been there for six months, assigned by Moscow to try and foment the war between the Sandinistas and the U.S.-backed Contras. It was not going well, in light of recent developments. Wearily, he looked at the Sandinista comandante of the zone, Miguel Horchiba Bonano. What to do about the comandante? he thought. Continue to work with him, or kill him and replace him with somebody he could trust? The comandante, he was certain, was up to something, acting on his own against the wishes of Moscow, who had backed Bonano with arms and training—up to this point. Moscow had made it clear that if caught by the CIA, Kubchkin was to kill himself before being interrogated. A confirmed Russian presence inside Nicaragua would be used as a propaganda tool by the Americans. Kubchkin wasn't anxious to stay in Nicaragua any longer than necessary.

Sweating, Bonano stood at attention in front of Kubchkin, silent, grim-faced. Kubchkin thought he had the look of a guilty man trying to hide something.

"Comandante, we seem to be having a serious problem to communicate lately. Can you adequately explain to my satisfaction what is going on at the garrison? I have heard rumors, very unsettling rumors, that demand my immediate attention. You have been summoned here to answer my questions and for the both of us to determine how we shall proceed against the Contras, led by *El Tigre*, in this zone."

"Of course, Major, you know of the recent shipment of arms that the CIA sent, or tried to send, to the Contras."

"Of course I know about that. I have my men everywhere in the zone, as you should well know. You were successful in capturing those weapons. I congratulate you on your victory. It is the CIA agents I am interested in that you have captured. I want them."

Bonano shook his head. "It is not so easy as that, Major."

Kubchkin felt himself tremble with suppressed rage. "If we cut off supplies and arms to you, Comandante, nothing will be so easy. We know there is an American troop buildup along the Honduran border. Could this country, Comandante, survive an American invasion and occupation, and a return to the former government of a Somoza-like dictator, an American puppet, without our assistance to prevent just such an invasion?"

Bonano held up a restraining hand. "Let me explain, Major. I believe that this CIA man, Major Ellis, can be a useful propaganda tool, for you and for Moscow and for the present government in Nicaragua. I must sit on him for the time being. My informant inside the Contra camp of this zone tells me four mercenaries have come here to free this Major Ellis. Do you understand the implications of such a mission as theirs?"

"*Nyet*, I do not follow you."

Bonano cleared his throat, his hands clasped behind

his back. "They are here to recapture this Major Ellis from us, thus stripping us of a useful propaganda tool in Major Ellis. Now, were we to capture these mercenaries instead, together with Ellis, we could prove to the world that the CIA has committed itself to hostile intentions against Nicaragua. The Americans, they would demand that their Congress cut all aid to the Contras, and in that event the Contras would cease to exist as a fighting unit. The revolution would then be a complete success. Nicaragua could belong to the Sandinistas without opposition."

Kubchkin nodded as if he understood. And he did understand. Bonano was in this for personal gain, hated the Russian and Cuban presence as much as he did the Americans and the CIA. Bonano was looking for a high place for himself in Managua. The SPETSNAZ major rubbed his jack-o'-lantern jaw, swatted at a fly. Bonano could end up proving himself a liability instead of an asset before they had annihilated the Contras in the zone. Kubchkin didn't need any more problems than he already had. Moscow was expecting results, and soon. Kubchkin knew he was expected to produce those results.

"There is a rumor that you are sitting on one million dollars American cash that was to be delivered from the CIA to the Contras fighting under *El Tigre*. Is this true?"

"*Sí*. It is true. I was not attempting to hide this fact from you. My feeling is that the money rightfully belongs to me and my fighting unit. The spoils of war, you understand."

Spoils of war. Kubchkin liked that. What he thought Bonano really meant to say was that "the money belongs to me." Corruption, Kubchkin knew, dictated the course of events in Latin America. Everybody in Nicaragua was lining their own pockets.

Kubchkin stood. He towered over Bonano by a full head. He squared his broad shoulders, saw the shadows of his SPETSNAZ commandos beyond the tent, flickering against the canvas as they patrolled his jungle outpost. The sun was beginning to set over the jungle, but it was still as hot as a sauna inside the tent.

Kubchkin was now following Bonano's line of thinking—indeed, was way ahead.

"Comandante, let me present to you what I believe is your intention. These mercenaries, they are here to free this Major Ellis, who was a top covert CIA man."

"*Sí.*"

"Very well. It is your intention, I believe, to lure these mercenaries, who are in collusion with *El Tigre* and his Contras, to the garrison, using this Major Ellis as bait."

"*Sí.* You understand. *Bueno.*"

Kubchkin shook his hand at Bonano, began pacing behind the comandante. "Not so fast, Comandante. I am trying to understand. You lure these mercenaries and *El Tigre* to the garrison, then what?"

"We kill them, of course, or at least kill the bulk of *El Tigre*'s force."

"You just let them walk right into the garrison?"

"My informant will provide them with the necessary information to allow them to believe that Major Ellis's recapturing will be easy. I intend to crush *El Tigre* and all of his men at the garrison. And capture the mercenaries, if possible. They will be your propaganda tools for Moscow to use. In turn, for helping bring this plan about, I ask to keep the one million dollars American, courtesy of the hated CIA. It will be put in the Sandinista war chest. A double blow to the CIA. It will be a most humiliating day for the CIA, don't you think? Particularly when the world discovers the truth about what the CIA was attempting to do in Nicaragua. Upscale the war by heavily arming and financing the Contras."

Kubchkin grunted, rubbing his chin. Bonano's plan, he decided, was not without merit. Despite whatever personal gains he had in mind for himself, the Comandante would serve the SPETSNAZ purpose there in Nicaragua. And that was to make the Americans look bad and show them up to the rest of the world as the true aggressors in Central America.

"Your plan, Comandante, just might work," the SPETSNAZ major said, and won an approving smile from Bonano. "However . . . I will go over details of the garrison raid you suspect will take place. My own SPETSNAZ commandos will trail the mercenaries and *El Tigre*'s forces through the jungle and into the garrison. I personally will be there to overlook the operation. It all has great potential, Comandante, great potential. If your plan works as you have envisioned, you may keep the CIA war chest intended to fall into the hands of the Contras. However . . . if this is just some smoke screen for you to send me and my men running off into the jungle to chase ghosts so that you make certain you keep that CIA money . . . hoping that we may meet an untimely demise . . . be warned . . . Moscow will not look favorably upon it. Do you understand?"

Bonano grinned, spread his hands. "I understand perfectly, Major. Miguel Horchiba Bonano, Comandante of the zone, is at your service, as always. I can be trusted, believe me."

Kubchkin didn't know what to make of the comandante, just looked at him and grunted. The man was either a fool or a man with a cunning, diabolical mind. Kubchkin decided he would just have to wait and see which it was.

"We shall see, Comandante. Come. We have a slaughter to plan."

The gunship landed at the edge of the jungle tree line. A tall man with dark aviator shades, tiger-striped camos, and a crew cut hopped out of the fuselage. He carried a holstered .45 Colt ACP on his hip.

He was simply known as the Iceman, or Iceman, but his mission in Central America wasn't so simple. He was there on CIA business. A terminate-with-extreme prejudice order to fulfill. Kill or be killed. No one knew him, of him, or about him. He was on his own. He knew he and twelve other men, ordered to carry out this operation, were the loneliest men on the face of the earth. About as lonely as the man they were going to kill. Major Ben Ellis.

With long strides, the Iceman strode away from the Huey gunship. The sun was beginning to set behind the rolling forested hills of Honduras, casting a brilliant crimson haze over the jungle. Through the pounding rotor wash, Iceman heard the familiar screech of wild birds, felt at ease. He was once again back in the jungle. Familiar turf. Just like his Special Forces days in Vietnam. But the real front at the moment, he knew, was hundreds of klicks away. In Nicaragua. Iceman was anxious to get there.

"I have been expecting you. Colonel Wallabee. United States Army."

Iceman looked at the tall, whip-lean man in the dark shades and green camos. Wallabee was probably a good man, Iceman decided, when it came down to doing things the standard military way. Iceman didn't have time to bullshit around with any government issues. Wallabee didn't offer his hand and Iceman didn't offer his.

"Uncle Sam's finest," Iceman grunted, and took the intelligence report, marked "top secret," from Wallabee's hand. "Inside your tent, Colonel."

Quickly, the Iceman read the intelligence report. Once they were inside the colonel's tent, the Iceman fired up an El Producto with a Zippo.

Iceman paced around the tent like a caged tiger, puffing on his stogie. "Who are these four men inside the target zone, Colonel?"

"We're not sure. My sources inside the zone say they are outsiders, rogue mercenaries, and they're not sure why they are there. They brought weapons and supplies to *El Tigre*'s Contra unit. Marched them from the Mosquito Coast southwest to San Pedro, which is less than a dozen klicks from the garrison holding Major Ellis. That much has been confirmed."

"No names."

"None that we can ascertain."

Iceman grunted. He didn't like loose ends. "Then they'll have to be terminated also."

"I hate having to work with you CIA types, but I've got my orders from upstairs."

"Right you do, Colonel. Explicit orders. Yours is not to reason why, mine is but to do or die. Now. Give me the layout on this gig."

Colonel Wallabee scowled for a moment, appeared set to say something contradictory, then just cleared his throat loudly and went on with his report. "A gunship will transport you and your men inside the target zone. You will secure your own firebase. One gunship will be allowed for you for your mission. The other gunship will be left at the firebase for your exfiltration once the mission is completed to your satisfaction. How you get out is your business. What happens after is your business, as you well know."

"My men. They're here?"

"Yeah. At the tent near the edge of the jungle. At the southeast quadrant. All unnecessary personnel have been removed from the area. Everything is secured on my end, as you requested. You're on your own, as of this moment. I don't know you. I haven't seen you. Personally, I despise these kinds of operations. One of our people gets caught doing what they've been ordered to do, and what does Langley do? They send in a goon squad to rub him out so they can cover their own asses. Christ. I hate this fucking so-called war. I wonder sometimes just what the hell it is we're doing down here."

"So do I. Fighting communism?" Iceman posed, and cracked a cold grin at the colonel.

"All I'm down here doing, mister, is training a few Contra rebels."

"Right, Colonel. Hear no evil, and like that. But you jump to do the Company's bidding."

"I jump, mister, because I want to see my pension."

"Okay, that's it on your end, Colonel. Get us those gunships and we're airborne. Good work."

"Right. Excuse me if I don't say thanks."

Tossing his cigar aside, Iceman left the tent, strode across the clearing, and entered the tent where he was told he would find his men. They were there. Sitting in hard-backed, fold-up wooden chairs. M16s slung around their shoulders. Commando daggers and machetes sheathed by their sides. Shades over their eyes. Hard, grizzled faces of combat veterans and mercenaries. Twelve guns in all. The Iceman's Dozen, he called them.

"All right, listen up," he addressed his dozen guns. "We're flying out tonight at 0100. You know the score. You know the mission. We go into the target zone. I'm passing around photos taken of four men, unknowns, but presumably in the zone to free the principal target, Major Ellis. We come across them, we kill them. We kill anything that moves. We don't leave behind a trace of what it was we were there to do. You people know me or of me, so you know I don't have time for any bullshit. If you fuck up, or fuck me up, I'll kill ya where ya stand. Life sucks, and all that, yeah. The CIA has no knowledge of us, even though you who do survive this operation will be drawing a paycheck from them. That's how it goes. We're expendables. Any questions?"

There were no questions. Good, Iceman thought. This should be a fairly simple termination. He knew them by name only, most of their names aliases, knew of their past performances in different branches of the service. They were handpicked by him and the Company's Special Operations Division. Some of them would die, he knew. He didn't care. All of them were simply nameless, faceless entities, there in Central America to sanitize a situation. No one would cry for them, bleed for them, or miss them when they were gone. They were all dead men walking. Life sucks, and all that.

"All right, then. Lock and load. We got us a payday to draw."

Chapter 8

Bad Zac Dillinger decided to hang back for the moment, check the situation out, sort out his thoughts, put a finger on the whole ball of crap, and give it either a plus or a minus. The situation stank, from beginning to now. They were all gathered inside a gutted building with jagged walls and no ceiling, another place reeking of death and decay. They were getting the final brief by *El Tigre* before heading out into the jungle to run down and raid the garrison overlorded by Attila the Hun. All of them, Dillinger believed, were in for the longest night of their lives, twenty-four hours ahead that would most definitely become somebody's eternity. The jungle beyond the rubble was alive with the caws of wild birds, the chirp and buzz of millions of insects, and the ever-present screech of the howler monkeys. It made Dillinger feel as if he was removed from the rest of the civilized world. Then he thought that he was stupid even to feel that way since he had never known civilized to begin with.

"These are my best and most trusted men and fighters," *El Tigre* told Eagle Force. "Don Juan, Poet, Rat Man, John Wayne, and Zorro. They will not let me nor you down. I trust them with my life."

"You might have to before this is over," Vic Gabriel told *El Tigre*. "What about the informant you mentioned? Any line on that yet?"

El Tigre shrugged. "With these matters it is hard to say. It is not a good thing, I know. We live with informants constantly down here. One day they just switch camps.

79

Who is to say why? Ideology? A loved one threatened by the opposition in some way?"

"Informants with shaky ideology may cost us our asses, *El Tigre*," Johnny Simms growled, giving the Tiger's best men a mean eyeballing. "Any rotten ones among your bunch, you know what will have to be done."

"*Sí*. It is expected. They will be killed on the spot. In time, this informant will show himself and he will be dealt with so that he is no more. A scorpion among us that we will crush. Now, you have told me what you wish to do," *El Tigre* said, looking at Vic Gabriel, who fired up a Marlboro. "Attila's garrison is exactly 11.5 kilometers due southwest of San Pedro. Through tough jungle. There is a main trail but we cannot risk it. A stream, an offshoot of the Escondido River, runs on a course parallel to the trail, and would bring us closest to the garrison at the eleventh kilometer. The Escondido and its offshoots, they are patrolled by gunboats, but much of the forest has been cleared out near the banks of the tributary for the soldiers to make it easier for them to patrol the zone. It would make the way easier for us, too."

"We go that route then," Gabriel said. "It goes without saying what has to happen to any patrols we run across."

"*Sí*. It goes without saying. Another ambush would cut our numbers even more seriously and could prove disastrous. I plan to leave behind a staggered column, checkpoints. We have two radio backpacks and we will leave one behind for the rearguard. The rear guard, they will watch and monitor our backs while we advance. I will take fifty men with us, if that is all right with you."

"Fine. What about the garrison itself?"

"A big place, almost as large in total area as San Pedro. Machine-gun nests along the ramparts on all points of the compass. A large courtyard. Perhaps two hundred enemy numbers there. Your friend, he would be held, most likely, in a cell belowground at the far southeast sector. A number of my men have been inside before. Tortured by Attila. Only three of them have escaped to tell about it."

Dillinger torched a stogie. Lolita was sitting on a pile of rubble near Gabriel. Damn, she was a looker, he thought, and could well appreciate how a man, even a man as strong-willed and ballsy as his friend Vic, could fall for that one and lose sight of his objective. What was the real story there? he wondered. Not that he really cared all that much, he was just a nosy SOB and liked to know the score on all things happening in his vicinity. And none of them knew the first thing about Vic's lover girl. She could definitely prove to be a fatal beauty to one or all of them, Dillinger thought. Obviously they were old lovers from Vic's days as a paramilitary operative for the Company, tracking down Michael Saunders, the murderer of his father. But there was something else going on, too, Dillinger could sense the heat between them. What? Had Vic just walked away from her years ago, disappeared without a trace, and left her to nurse her bruised female vanity and ego and curse the day he was born? Had she argued with her old lover that she wanted to come along on this killhunt and Vic had objected but finally relented? She looked like she could handle herself in a firefight, or any kind of fight for that matter. She sat perched on the rock, M16 slung around her shoulder, big commando dagger sheathed by her side, like one of them, a predatory animal hunting prey. There was some raw power in her presence, a savagery about her that fascinated Dillinger. But, hell, no, he wasn't about to make any moves on his buddy's woman. First of all, the ex-PI determined, she didn't seem the type to allow straying hands to grope for her. She would just as soon crack him right across the face as look at his ugly mug. Vic would probably just as soon kick his ass, too. They already had enough problems without him acting like some dog in heat on this killhunt.

Okay, the situation was definitely a minus. Had started out a minus. But the three of them, Dillinger knew, were doing this for Vic. Nicaragua, hell, most all of Central America, he knew, was a festering blight on the rest of the Western Hemisphere. Dictators and peasants and appalling poverty. Drugs and gunrunning and every vice and form of corruption under the sun. And the East and West slugging it out with each other over who controlled the whole mess. Somebody else could have it; Dillinger didn't want any part of it. The ex-PI from sunny Fort Lauderdale just wanted to wrap this up and get the hell out of Nicaragua. Much easier said than done. The situation was growing more complicated with each half klick they put behind them.

"You know how I plan to do this, *El Tigre*," Gabriel said, blowing funnels of smoke out his nostrils like a dragon. "A full-scale frontal assault. Judging from the sounds of what this garrison is like, it won't be easy, but it can be done. I'm here to tell you, we've tackled numbers every bit as tough and large as we'll be up against. Whatever we encounter along the way in the form of a Sandinista is left behind, dead meat for the jaguar and condor. By now, we know that Attila knows we're coming. That makes it harder on us. We probably won't get the element of surprise. Attila might even be waiting for us as soon as we set foot out of San Pedro. We should be prepared for a fight to the death. I want your men to understand that. If they can't commit themselves to that, I don't want them along."

El Tigre, a grim smile cutting his bearded face, looked from his men, all of whom were nodding, to Gabriel. "We would have this no other way, hombre. We are here for the express purpose of ridding the zone of them, or falling dead where we fight."

"Good. Then it's set. If you'll give me a few minutes with my men?"

El Tigre nodded. The Contras left. Lolita stayed behind, and she became the unfocused focal point of the four commandos. There was the thick heat of tension among the men of Eagle Force. Dillinger sensed it, knew Gabriel would have to address it. The commander of Eagle Force would have to rid the three of them of their fears that an old love interest had taken some kind of priority over them and their mission.

"Lolita," Gabriel said, and looked at his commandos in turn. "This is Zac Dillinger, also known as Bad Zac. He's a dirty old man, so watch yourself," he said, cracking a grin.

Dillinger chuckled and nodded at Lolita. "Don't believe everything this guy tells ya about me," he gruffed, grinning. "He's a liar, a cheat, and a scoundrel, as you probably already well know, you poor girl. I'm really just an angel at heart, señorita, so you may have to excuse this dirty old man and broken-down war-horse on occasion if I run my foul mouth too much. Problem is I was an abused kid, so bear with me if I act like I need a lot of attention."

Gabriel softly shook his head, looked at Simms and Boolewarke. "Johnny Simms and Henry van Boolewarke. Johnny boy and Dutch. Two more abused kids who need lots of attention," he said, grinning to himself. "They're good men and all of us go the distance for each other, no questions asked. All right, she's part of the group now. She doesn't want any special privileges, or any special attention, if you catch my drift. She can hold her own."

"They look like tough hombres," Lolita said. "I believe the Sandinistas, they have more to fear from us than we from them."

"Let's hope," Gabriel said. "Give us a minute?"

"*Sí,*" Lolita said, nodding, and left the four commandos alone.

Gabriel fired up another smoke, heaved a breath, drew a deep drag. "It's a long story, so don't ask. I don't feel like talking about it now. We've got a mission to tackle. I almost wish now I hadn't brought you three along. Get your asses killed for my mission of mercy."

"Stop feeling sorry for yourself, old man," Dutch growled.

"Ditto," Simms added. "We wouldn't have had it any other way, and you know it. 'Sides, what the hell were the three of us gonna do back on the island? Sunbathe, drink rum all day, and fuck with each other?"

Dillinger laughed heartily. "That sums it up in a nutshell, VG. We're with you all the way. And I promise . . . I'll keep my hands and my eyes to myself."

"Lying sack of shit, you," Dutch growled.

Gabriel chuckled. "You'd better, Bad One. She'll cut your ass up good. And then she'll cut my ass up for having such warped taste in buddies."

"I'm a believer," Dillinger said. "Say no more."

"Listen," Gabriel said, turning serious. "I'd never lose my head over a woman, any woman, if that's what you've been worried about. I think you know that already, it just doesn't hurt to hear it. The mission comes first. Getting us out alive and in one piece is also top priority. Enough said."

"'Nuf said," Johnny Simms echoed. "And you," he said, looking at Dillinger, "I'll be sure to keep your ass in line when the señorita's around."

"Listen to your ass," Dillinger growled. "That's like sending a thief to guard the queen's jewels. Christ. The shit I gotta put up with."

Gabriel smiled to himself. "All right, now that everything's back to normal. Let's get ready to head out and greet Attila the Hun."

Back to business, Dillinger thought, and felt a great sense of relief. Vic had just put their fears to rest.

"I overheard what you said."

Vic Gabriel stood in the twilight gloom just beyond a heap of rubble. He looked deep into Lolita's eyes, saw that she was trying her damnedest to hide her pain and hurt. No matter what else she was, she was still a woman, and she needed to feel special, even under these grim circumstances. Moments ago, she had pulled him away and over into the shadows without his men seeing them go off by themselves. Gabriel listened to the encroaching night, the sounds of animal and insect life all around them, clawing at their senses from the forbidding darkness of the jungle.

"Lolita, I . . ."

She put a finger on his lips. "I understand. You do not need to explain yourself to me. You must let your men know they are not threatened by us, or how we might feel for each other. Whatever is to happen, I accept it. If one of us is to die . . ."

"Don't say that. Listen . . . I . . . I . . ."

"You what?"

She smiled that all-knowing smile that he remembered from so long ago. It was as if she could read his thoughts before he said them.

"You will take me away from here when this is over?"

"Yeah," Vic Gabriel said, and meant it. "I will. We have an island in the Caribbean all to ourselves. A beautiful place. A quiet place. White sand and sunshine. It's peaceful there. I want you to come there with me when this is finished."

"Would your men accept it? Would they accept me?"

"They would if I asked them to. Yeah. Don't talk about death. You might jinx us," he said, and tried a smile he didn't feel.

"Are you asking me to go to this place with you?"

"I am."

"I accept. Kiss me."

And he kissed her. When he pulled away, tasting the sweet warmth of her lips still on his mouth, he told her, "We'll make it out of here. I promise."

"I want that, Vic Gabriel. I don't ever want to lose you again. Never."

But some terrible feeling welled up in Vic Gabriel's gut as he stood there looking at her. He didn't know what it was, but the promises he'd just made sounded hollow in his ears, like they were voiced from miles away, from somebody else. Not that he didn't intend to follow up on his promise. He just didn't like the feeling of foreboding he had. It nagged at him, and as she smiled, and walked away to leave him alone, standing in the shadows of the jungle, he felt himself pulled back in time.

To a place in his long-lost, almost forgotten youth, where death had surrounded him and begun this unwitting journey across an entire ocean, thousands of miles away.

The present removed him to another time, another battle.

He was pulled back, locked in the past.

Remembering.

Frozen in the death struggle of so long ago.

Screaming demons poured out of the crimson mist.

Young Vic Gabriel knew he was going to die. The why, when, where, or how didn't even matter anymore. He was checking out. It was that ugly, that simple, but suddenly it was not at all that frightening. It would even come as a relief. Death, he thought for a split second, sure seemed pretty simplistic in its ugly brutal unforgiving finality. Knowing that it's coming can give a man a mighty strange peace inside, he decided, an acceptance of the end without bitterness or anger. Young Vic Gabriel almost smiled. Almost, except that his damn face hurt too much. The final curtain call, he thought.

It would all come crashing down around him in a rain of bullets and blood.

No more pain.

No more worries.

Nothing . . . but . . .

Vic Gabriel stood on legs that felt as if they were made of macaroni. They ripped out of the jungle, a thousand and one cannibals with fangs. A million demons with flaming talons.

Screaming at the top of his lungs, high on one last surge of adrenaline, Gabriel backpedaled up the steps of the temple, squeezing the trigger of his M60, sweeping the big chattering man-eater, left to right, right to left.

Dropping them in shrieking death.

Chewing up the enemy and sending them on their way.

He felt the slugs tearing into him.

Tasted the blood washing over his face.

And Buddha, laughing behind him, grinning that stupid grin on his piggish face.

The jungle tree line wavered in Gabriel's crimson sight. The roar of the man-eater filled his ears. Cursing, screaming tore across no-man's-land as bodies piled up on each other and twitching limbs danced in the symphony of brutal death.

At first, he didn't even see the chopper. It was just some blurry thing in the periphery of his vision, rolling along over a tree line that coiled and rippled and constricted like a million venomous snakes.

Exhausted, Gabriel pitched on his back.

They charged up the steps, but he hosed them down, sent them tumbling back down the steps and bowling into each other. He tasted their blood and bile and guts spewing over his face as he tore them up with endless rounds of death and mutilation. They were that close, right on top of him.

Gunship. He recognized the whapping bleat, hell, felt

he hot rotor wash against his face like a breath of life.
Renewed strength and hope surged through him, steeled his
will to survive. He heard the familiar and god-awful-
pleasing snarl of M60s and miniguns unleashed on the
boiling cesspool of enemy humanity.

Vietcong dropped to no-man's-land by the dozens.

Shrill screams ripped the dawn sky asunder.

Gabriel felt hot shell casings battering his face as he
mercilessly poured death over the charging Cong. He tried
to stand, then slipped in a slick pool of blood. His own? Or
the blood of the countless Cong heaped up on the steps at
his feet?

He didn't care.

The sky spun.

The gunship faded in and out of his sight.

Dawn turned black.

The next thing he knew, hands were clawing into his
wounds, and he was being draped over somebody's shoulder. He spat up blood, and groaned.

He heard his voice echo, "Wh-who . . . wh-who . . ."

"Relax, son. We're taking you home."

Son? No. It can't be. His father?

He felt himself bounce all over a pair of brawny
shoulders that felt as if they were carved out of mountain
rock.

"Captain Ben Ellis, son, at your service. 101st Airborne. Don't say a word until I get you the hell outta here."

The rotor wash shrieked over Gabriel. The rotor
blades sounded like giant buzz saws as he was gently laid
down in the fuselage and looked up. Through a haze, he
found the face of the man he assumed had carried him off
the temple steps. Captain Ben Ellis. 101st Airborne. If
nothing else about this moment, he would remember that
name. He owed the guy. Owed him big.

Captain Ben Ellis. Owed him his life for snatching him
out of the bowels of hell.

And hell was exactly what young Vic Gabriel saw in
the distance. Countless bodies, strewn across no-man's-
land. Mangled sacks littering the temple steps.

And that damnable grinning pig face of Buddha. Vic

Gabriel didn't have anything against any man's religion, but for some reason, Buddha looked like the face of the devil to him at that moment.

"Get some rest."

Vic Gabriel looked up at the grizzled face of Captain Ben Ellis. "How . . . how . . ."

"I said, get some rest, son. I'll explain when I get you back."

Explain? Explain what? What was there to explain? Somebody had fucked up. Or had somebody purposely fucked up?

A hundred questions, none of them good, danced through the pain in Vic Gabriel's head.

All he knew was that he was alive.

Alive when so many other good men had died. And for what? God in heaven, he thought, for what?

Chapter 9

Twelve big shadows boiled up out of the blackness. All twenty of the sentries left behind by *El Tigre* to guard San Pedro were cut down by swift silent blades. Short sharp grunts rang away from the rubble and echoed death gurgles in the night. Cold razor-sharp steel pierced hearts or sliced throats. Each kill was perfectly timed and executed so that the bulk of the Contra sentries died at the same instant. Their blood ran in the dirt, mingling streams of dark crimson to be sucked on by greedy buzzing flies. Lifeless figures dropped, and a dozen grim-faced men, toting M16s and M60 machine guns, converged on the village square. One of the shadows kicked a mongrel clear across the street, slamming its emaciated frame into a mound of rubble. The dog whimpered and retreated into the darkness, as if sensing that once again death had come to San Pedro.

Colonel Hank Tilton walked down the center of the street like a conquering hero. He felt anything but a hero. He was still sweating, still hating Nicaragua, still smoking a cigar, and still craving to get his hands on that million dollars American, courtesy of the CIA. He was eager to get his hands on that bundle and get the hell out of Nicaragua. Once clear and free of Central America, he would set himself up nicely on a Caribbean island of his choosing. Of course, the money would have to be divided up, but in war there are always casualties, and if he played his cards right, it might all come down to a three- or a two-way split. If he played his hand real good and kept a big ace in the hole, he

would be the only one left sitting at the poker table, h
thought. His big ace was his .45 Colt.

Tilton ignored the pleas and cries of the women a
several of his men descended on them. They deserved
little R & R, after all, he figured. The Nicaraguan wenche
would be serviced by fine young military men, he though
and then be put out of his men's misery with a bulle
through their peasants' brains. He knew his men didn
want to be adding to the burgeoning population of Centra
America by fathering illegitimate Nicaraguan brats.

And Colonel Hank Tilton, puffing contentedly on hi
stogie, strode into the church of San Pedro. He saw th
candlelight beyond the rows of splintered pews, saw th
rubble heaped around the altar, and laughed to himse
when he saw the huge cross suspended over the altar
These people were nothing but pagans to Tilton, less tha
animals. How could they believe in a divine being? As sur
as he was standing there smoking Havana's finest, Go
hadn't smiled on them. These people lived worse tha
dogs. In squalor and disgusting poverty. In filth, wallowin
in their own piss and shit. Life had taken one huge shit o
the miserable souls of Nicaragua, he thought, and they ha
become the shit. Shit only needed to be shoveled out of th
way before you stepped in it. By God, he was there do t
some shoveling.

Followed into the church by Willard the Beast, Rosco
Stilts, Paneras the Panamanian, and Jocko, Tilton, M1
poised and ready to cut down anything that moved, heade
for the altar. He stepped on something. He looked dow
and saw the something was a pained face twisted inside
spool of bloodstained bandages. Tilton relieved himself o
that face, and as the wounded Contra hissed and curse
him, the colonel zipped his pants up and shot the man i
the temple, point-blank.

Hank Tilton didn't have time for peasants, but hi
shovel was always ready, by God.

"*Madre de Dios! Madre de Dios!* What is the meanin
of this?"

Tilton gave his troops a curt nod. Quickly, like shark

zeroing in on bloody chum, they raced into the back of the church. They knew what to do.

"Relax, padre," Tilton told Father Hercado.

The colonel rolled up on Hercado, stuck the muzzle of his M16 under the Catholic priest's jaw.

Autofire blistered the night. Screams tore through the church. Moments later, Tilton's men hustled six nuns in various states of undress out onto the altar. There, they forced them to their knees at gunpoint. They laughed, spat on the nuns, and made obscene remarks.

"This is an outrage! I demand to know what you are doing?"

"I want some information, padre." Tilton blew smoke in Hercado's face. "I ain't got time for bullshit. You talk, I spare the rest of your village. I got a *sí* on that?"

Hercado seemed to wrestle with his decision, then finally nodded. "What do you want?"

"I saw a rather large patrol of men pull outta here a little more than an hour ago. Where were they going?"

"How should I know? I am not a solider. I am a man of God! I do not get involved in the devil's bidding."

A shrill female scream, then autofire raked the murk in the doorway behind Tilton.

"This is an outrage! You can't do this!"

"But I am, padre, I am. Let's just say at the moment, I am who I am. I got a million bucks out there and a lowlife spick shithead named Banana is sitting on it. I want to know who those four mercenaries are and where they're headed. C'mon, padre. You got eyes and ears. You see things. You hear things." A grim smile cut Tilton's lips. "You're a man of God, after all. You should be everywhere."

"You will pay dearly for your blasphemy."

"So sue me. You talk, old fuck, or you die and pay for your blasphemy against me, right here, right now."

Hercado clenched his teeth. "You spare our lives?"

"I look like a man who would break his word?"

"You look like what you are. A murderer."

An uncontrollable rage seized Tilton. He chopped Hercado over the head with his M16, driving him to his

knees. Father Hercado ignored the blood streaming down
his face as Tilton leveled the M16 on him.

"One last chance, padre."

"There were four of them, *sí*. Mercenaries. Here on
their own. This is what I hear. They came here to rescue a
friend of one of them. A Major Ben Ellis, I am told. He is
being held at the garrison."

"And that's where they were headed?"

Hercado looked away from Tilton, as if ashamed he had
given in to him, and nodded.

"No mention of any money that Banana is sitting on?"

"What money? I hear nothing about any money. If
there is money there, it is blood money, meant to continue
this war."

"Right, right, blood money." Tilton drew on his cigar,
washed a thick cloud of smoke over Hercado. He thought
about what he'd seen through his infrared binoculars while
surveying the village before he'd made his grand entrance.
He remembered seeing what he figured was the commander of the four mercs talking to a woman. There
seemed to have been a strain between the commander and
the woman, but there also seemed to be a bond between
them. The woman had left with the Contra patrol. She
could prove to be a key somehow in whatever plan he chose
to initiate against the Contra patrol. A bargaining chip,
perhaps. He was going to change his original plan, go ahead
and try to hook up with the Contra patrol and storm
Banana's garrison. It seemed the best way to get the million
dead presidents in one piece. All right, then, the woman
had to play a vital role.

"One last question, padre. The woman. The head
merc. What's the story there?"

Hercado grimaced, looked set to spit on Tilton's boots,
then answered him, "I understand they were lovers from
years ago. The woman, her name is Lolita Armandez. She
had a son by one of them. He is dead now."

Interesting, Tilton thought. There were some real
possibilities in his new plan, after all.

"Now what?" Willard the Beast called out from the
altar.

Tilton looked long and hard at the six nuns. He had always thought nuns were ugly old fat women, but he saw these nuns were young and pretty damned good-looking from where he stood. Hell, he decided, his men needed some more R & R before heading out into the bush. It would sharpen their combat senses, he told himself.

Tilton looked down at Hercado and grinned. "Sorry, Father. I guess I lied. Give my regards to Jesus."

Hercado opened his mouth to say something, but Tilton cored a 5.56mm slug through that vented maw.

"Do what you want with the nuns," Tilton told his men. "But be quick about it." Wheeling, he found two more of his troops standing in the doorway. "Kill 'em all. Fuck it. Let God sort 'em out."

As Tilton walked out into the dark street of San Pedro, the sounds of slaughter roared over him. He felt good, though, big, tall, strong, invincible. He puffed on his cigar and watched as his men mowed down anything and everything that moved. Dogs, chickens, cats, burros. It didn't matter, and he didn't give a damn. San Pedro was just another sore on the pimple of the ass of Nicaragua, which was nothing but a festering wound on the free world. God, how he wanted that million. Damn, how he wanted to get the hell out of Nicaragua and forget this place even existed.

Willard the Beast, wearing a smug grin and zipping up his pants, strode up behind Tilton. "What's the plan, Colonel?"

Tilton stopped in the middle of the street. Slowly, he drew down on a mongrel scampering across the street and drilled a three-round burst into the dog's hide. A young boy, crying for his dog, burst out of the shadows and flung himself over his dog. Tilton crucified dog and boy together with another three-round burst.

Tilton puffed on his stogie. "Been a change of plan, soldier. We might have to force the vanguard to team up with us."

"How's that?"

"Shut up. I'm thinking, I'm thinking."

But the only thing Colonel Hank Tilton was thinking

about was a million dollars American, courtesy of the CIA. And how he would keep it all to himself.

Vic Gabriel crouched in the brush. His commandos, *El Tigre* and his most trusted fighters, a dozen other Contras, and Lolita gathered around him. Ahead, Gabriel saw the generator-powered light washing a soft white hue over the short wharf. Two gunboats were moored by a small shack. He counted ten armed shadows. And there were twenty-three of them, soon to be minus one in a few moments. Gabriel trusted Lolita to do her part when the fighting went down, but for some reason he was still reluctant to let her do her share of the killing. He didn't want her hurt, then realized that desire in itself could be lethal. It might cause him to keep a concerned eye on her and deflect his attention away from the killing fields. Hell with it, he told himself. He'd take each moment, each step through the jungle as it came, forget the risk and danger to his woman, and ride out the thunder. It was the only sensible thing to do.

"All right," Gabriel told them, "we take down those soldiers. We move in on the garrison by gunboat. It's the quickest and maybe the safest way. All of you come with me, but you," he said to Lolita, "go back and wait with the others."

She opened her mouth to say something, but Gabriel sharply ordered, "Don't argue."

She didn't. Silently, she melted back into the jungle.

They were almost ninety minutes out of San Pedro. The going had been slow and arduous, as Gabriel had taken his commandos on ahead for recon and to be sure their advance would be paved without the possibility of an ambush. They had lost valuable time.

Now the time seemed perfect for the first lethal strike against the guns of Attila.

The jungle was dark and thick around them. The sounds of animal and insect life would mask their approach to the wharf.

"That one, I hope she is not trouble for you, hombre."

Gabriel gave *El Tigre* a hard look. "Not so long as she does what she's told to do."

El Tigre smiled to himself. "And here I thought all American men let their women wear the pants."

Bad Zac Dillinger grunted. "Not ones with any balls, pal."

Gabriel put Lolita out of his mind. The bulk of *El Tigre*'s force was a half klick back down the trail. The rear guard was secured.

"All right, let's do it," Vic Gabriel breathed, and moved out into the black night of the shrieking jungle.

Lolita Armandez knew this was not a situation where she could indulge herself to nurse hurt feelings. It was a time for survival, to steel herself for what she knew would be a life-or-death struggle for herself, as well as for the others. Attila the Hun was one of the most vicious comandantes in all of Nicaragua. It was Attila's unit that had claimed the life of her son. Like Gabriel, she, too, had a stake in seeing Bonano dead.

Silently, the vines and brush tearing at her fatigues, M16 poised and fanning the darkness around her, she moved through the jungle. Bats fluttered overhead. Howler monkeys danced through the canopy above her. Mosquitoes and other insects buzzed around her face. Sweat burned into her eyes. Long ago, she had learned how to move through the jungle, swiftly, quietly. Roll with it, not fight it. Blend in with it, and use the jungle as it presented itself to your advantage. Not bull through it with reckless abandon, as if you were desperate to get out of it and be at your objective. Feel your way through it, anticipate obstacles, and what you couldn't feel or see, you sensed.

As much as she tried not to, she still resented Gabriel for sending her back. Not because she felt she had been humiliated in front of the others. Not because she was a woman and she had no place on the killing fields and this would appear to be the implication of his order. No, she was worried about Gabriel's safety. The only way she could make certain he would stay alive was to be right there by his side. She obeyed his order to fall back—this time. But next time, and for the duration of the killhunt, she would be by his side.

No, it was not easy, being told by her lover to go back and wait with the others for their return. But she understood. He was in a position where his word had to be the ultimate authority, where his decisions could mean life or death, and he had to be obeyed or lose face among the ranks. He was still the same strong-willed take-charge type of man. A warrior who demanded the most of his abilities, and likewise expected the same of others. He gave trust and loyalty to comrades, because he expected the same in return. In their type of war, where death faced them down constantly, it was the only real thing that existed among them, perhaps the only thing that even really mattered. He had not changed over the years, she thought; then again, nobody ever really does.

Nothing ever really changes. Especially Nicaragua.

She often wondered how different life could have been if she'd gone off to Honduras to the university, or perhaps even something simpler, like waitressing at some fine hotel or restaurant in Managua or Tegucigalpa. But life wouldn't have been that much different, she decided. She would have still been restless, yearning to be with the people of her village, the peasants, the small ones who were being consumed by the ravages of the war, who were being trampled in the name of revolution and progress. In some small way her life might have been made more secure had she removed herself from the war. But a son had changed that forever. A son, though now dead because of the war. Her son's death had also changed how she felt about the future. After his death during one of Attila's raids on San Pedro, she had determined that she would fight on the Contra side for whatever should be the rest of her life. The largest part of her had died the day her son was killed.

Now, though, she felt alive again. Alive because the father of her son was back in Nicaragua. Vic Gabriel had promised to take her away to his island, away from Nicaragua, away from the war forever. He was not a man who broke promises. But would she be cheating herself somehow, cheating the oppressed people under the Sandinista regime, by bailing out and leaving her country of birth for good, throwing down her arms for a life of relative ease with her lover? She wasn't sure. Time would tell her that. Her life with Gabriel would decide that for her.

She was surprised that she felt no bitterness or anger toward Vic Gabriel, the father of her son. How could she? Love, she knew, was not bitterness or anger. She accepted Gabriel for what he was—a soldier of fortune, but an honest man with ideals and principles, a man who would be loyal to those he cared for until his last breath. Now that she knew the truth about why he had left her, it made the past easier to live with. And the present held a promise of a future for her with him.

Lolita Armandez decided she had plenty to live for. Where there had been despair, there was now hope. Where there had been death, there was now life.

She crouched in the brush to catch her breath, bracing her back against a tree. She looked back from where she had come. There was no sign of Gabriel and the others, not even a fracture of light from the targeted Sandinista wharf breaking through the dense foliage. She figured she was somewhere halfway between Gabriel and the rear guard. Sitting alone in the dark bowels of the jungle, a barrage of animal and insect noise swarming over her, made her feel small and vulnerable. She realized she was afraid, but only because she had a few moments to herself to think about it.

She was about to say a prayer for her safety and the safe return of Gabriel and the others when an arm suddenly wrapped around her throat. The M16 slipped from her grasp as she clawed at the arm, then she felt the cold steely edge of a knife pressed against the side of her face, and became utterly still.

"Scream, call out, and I'll slice that pretty face of yours up into a bloody mask. Got me, señorita?"

Shadows loomed over her from out of the darkness. Armed shadows. Three shadows.

"Stand. Slow."

She did as she was told. She found herself facing an enormous fat man. Like some obscene beacon in the night, the fat man's cigar tip glowed, an orange eye, as he puffed on the smoke. He stuck his sweaty face close to her nose, and she smelled the stink of smoke and body odor on him and almost gagged.

"What do you want?"

The fat man grinned around his cigar. "Couple of things. First we go back and take care of your rear guard. Then, my lovely little señorita, you become my bargaining chip for your boyfriend. Now, you scream or call out and alert him, I'll kill him and his buddies. Then you'll be out here, all alone. Just you and me and my men. I'll have my way with you first, then turn you over to my men . . . if you force my hand. You gonna cooperate?"

With hatred, she looked into the fat man's eyes. "*Sí,*" she spat.

She felt the life shrivel up inside her. Silently she cursed this fat man.

Where there had been hope, there was now despair. Where there had been life, there was now surely going to be death.

Chapter 10

Vic Gabriel wasn't afforded the luxury of choosing the moment to strike. The sentry seemed to sense something wrong, sense something out there in the jungle, and called the moment, urged on his own moment of death. The sentry was scanning the blackness, AK47 poised to fire, when blackness took him for good.

Like a panther lunging out of the brush, the ex–Special Forces warrior gutted the sentry with his Ka-Bar as he stepped off the planks. A sharp grunt, a burst of blood from his gaping mouth as Gabriel slid the commando dagger free just below his breastbone, and the sentry toppled, ramrod stiff in death. Swift-moving shadows—Simms, Dillinger and Boolewarke—surged past the commander of Eagle Force, bounded onto the wharf. They knew the drill, they had done it before. Lightning fast, no wasted motion, swift, brutal, and final.

More shadows, this time *El Tigre* and his soldiers, rolled onto the wharf, trailing the spearhead of steel death in the guise of Eagle Force.

A trio of heavy blades flashed for an instant in the glow of generator-powered light. Those same three blades slashed and gutted, sliced and skewered.

A voice yelled out in Spanish, and a figure boiled out of the doorway. With a three-round burst, Gabriel chopped that guy up and sent him reeling back into the gunboat HQ.

El Tigre and his men raced down the wharf, their M16s stuttering and dropping targets as the knife-kills splashed into the stream. Like dominoes, the Sandinistas fell, pirouetting off the wharf and crashing into the water. They never even got off a shot.

It was quick, and lethally efficient. Gabriel was impressed at how smoothly the kills went down, at how good *El Tigre* and his men had again proven themselves to be.

Then a shadow appeared on the bow of one of the two gunboats moored at the end of the dock. That shadow cut loose with a mounted .50-caliber machine gun. Slugs raked the wharf, spitting splinters and gouging up strips of plank as the tracking line of fire ripped into three of *El Tigre's* men.

"*Bastardo!*" *El Tigre* roared, and, crouched, defying the line of slugs stitching toward him, triggered his M16 on full-auto slaughter. "*Hijo de la chingada!*"

Gabriel flung himself into the HQ doorway, a hurricane of slugs peppering his position, wood fragments stinging his face like a dozen vicious scorpions. Together with his commandos and *El Tigre*, Gabriel washed a tidal wave of 5.56mm slugs over the .50-caliber wiseguy. Sparks showered the Sandinista gunner and a beehive of slugs violently ricocheted off the protective turret. Then the guy's head, unprotected by metal, erupted in a goreburst of blood and brain muck.

Quickly, Gabriel checked his own commandos, glad to find them breathing and in one piece. As if they knew the drill themselves, and Gabriel knew they did, a half dozen of *El Tigre's* finest boarded the gunboats. Two three-round bursts rang out in the night, and two bodies were flung overboard to their watery grave.

El Tigre, his face flushed with anger over losing several of his men, strode up beside Gabriel. "We are lucky, hombre, that there are no more Sandinistas in the immediate vicinity. I know the zone well. There are no more gunboat stations. No more Sandinistas should be within several miles of here."

"We hope," Gabriel growled.

Then the night offered up still another ugly surprise, and all hope was dashed in the following moments.

Distant autofire seemed to split the darkness around the wharf with a thunderous death knell of impending doom for all of them. Gabriel and his commandos and *El Tigre* were rooted to the wharf for a long moment, staring off into the jungle, as if deciding what to do, as if waiting for the enemy to come charging at them from out of the blackness of the jungle. The rear guard, Gabriel knew, was engaged in a fierce firefight. And Lolita had gone back there on his orders. Dammit . . . if . . . if something happened to her . . . after finding her again after all these years. After knowing what he knew about her and the son she had borne by him . . .

"Looks like our troubles have only begun," Bad Zac Dillinger growled. "The fucks must've crept up on us. Must've been watching us and followed us out of San Pedro."

"Comandante Gringo!"

Wheeling, Gabriel saw the radio backpack man running down the wharf. The receiver crackled with a strange voice, a gloating voice tinged with an accent that sounded pure Georgia cracker to Gabriel.

"Hey, you, big guy, the one called Gabriel."

Fear marched an icy hand up and down Gabriel's spine. Feeling the eyes boring into him from up and down the wharf, Gabriel took the radio headset.

"Tough guy, listen up!"

And Gabriel listened to the screams and the autofire as it echoed over the radio headset. The thud and thwack of bullets drilling into flesh and bone, the screams of men dying in fear and agony.

"Tough guy, Gabriel, this is the colonel here. I got a little proposition for you. As you can hear, your rear guard just got wiped out and I only lost one guy. My boys—and I'm here to tell ya, I'm mighty proud of 'em—took out about ten of *El Tigre's* rear watchers with blades before they even had a chance to piss themselves. Guess you just done the same at that gunboat station. They're good, damn good, my boys. The rest was easy. Quick bursts of M16 fire, like you just heard. Something else I want you to hear. So listen good, and weigh your options. You ain't got but one."

God, no, Gabriel thought, and feared the worst.

His worst fear dawned on him in grim reality a second later as Lolita's voice was transmitted.

"Gabriel, I'm sorry, they came out of nowhere . . . they—"

"That's enough, sweet thing, you done just fine. All right, tough guy. I'm coming down there for a little chat with you, some of my boys and me, that is. Suggest you hold your fire, if you value your girlfriend's, uh . . . ass. And a nice ass she has, I'm here to tell ya."

Harsh-sounding laughter.

The connection was severed.

Vic Gabriel let the headset fall from his hands. Rage threatened to overpower him. He felt the questioning stares digging into the back of his head. He looked at his commandos. He could sense the fury in *El Tigre*, the despair. They were waiting for him to call the next shot. There was no shot to call. He could do nothing but wait, and watch, and hope.

"I want everybody to hold their fire," Vic Gabriel said.

And the night seemed to weigh down upon his shoulders as he felt the air lock up in his throat. Weigh down upon him with an oppressive fear.

Miguel Horchiba Bonano didn't mind being known in the zone as Attila the Hun. In fact, he liked the title. He knew very little about the history of the Huns, but he knew the very name of Attila conjured up images of mass slaughter, pillaging, rape, and conquest in even the most uneducated of minds. That was enough. And it was surely enough that he was feared in the zone. Attila the Hun, he thought, and felt a warm stab of pride. That was what he was. A Hun. The greatest Hun of all. A warrior. A conqueror of worlds.

He stood at the open window of his command HQ, staring out across the sprawling courtyard. Generator-powered klieg lights lit the corners of the garrison on all points of the compass. Sentries patrolled the ramparts. Jeeps and transport trucks heaped with fuel and ammo sat like dark blocks near the weapons depot. The jungle was alive in the night with the ever-present screech of the howler monkeys.

He knew they were coming, but he was prepared.

He heard the scuffling from behind and turned. Major Ben Ellis, stripped to the waist and wearing the punishment of his captivity with defiance, was flung into the room by two AK47-toting guards.

"Ah, Major Ellis. Good of you to come."

"Cut with the bad jokes, Bonano. What do you want now?"

"*Nada, nada.*" Slowly, his hands clasped behind his back, Bonano walked out in front of his desk. The shark's-teeth necklace rattling, he stooped over a large trunk. Opening the trunk, he showed the major the spoils of war. Stack after stack of one-hundred-dollar bills, stamped with the benign face of Benjamin Franklin, stared up at Ellis.

"So? You brought me here to gloat?"

Bonano chuckled. He was beginning to like the major, he thought. The major had balls, had endured terrible punishment that Bonano wasn't sure even most of his own men could withstand.

"I brought you here to tell you something, Major. I have been informed by a closely guarded source inside Honduras that a raid is being staged on the garrison. A raid by CIA assassins. I believe this raid will take place sometime around dawn this morning, if my source is correct, and he has never been wrong before. I have been informed that twelve men are coming to wipe out this garrison, kill me, and kill you. You, Major, though, I have been informed, are the principal target. You have become a definite liability to your country. I believe you understand all this, how something like this goes." Bonano watched the major's expression closely. No hint of emotion. So the major had expected someone to come after him and kill him.

"Can you imagine that?" Bonano continued, closing the lid on the trunk of money with a loud thud. "Twelve men? Against two hundred? It seems impossible, but who knows, with their Yankee arrogance and their lust to live to

claim their money for such a mission, I am sure they wil
make a good accounting of themselves.

"Not only that, a most hated enemy of mine, a man by
the name of *El Tigre* is also in the zone. Four mercenaries
of undetermined origin and even more undetermined
scruples are allied with this man who calls himself the
Tiger. It would be foolish to send my men out into the
jungle to track them down and meet them head-on when al
I have to do is wait for them to come to me. Do not worry,
Major, I will keep you alive at all costs. Your life is very
valuable to me. There are Russians in the zone also." Again,
no change of expression on the major's face. But, of course,
Ellis would have already known that Russians were in
Nicaragua. Life seemed to be holding very few surprises
these days in Central America.

"So? A big fight to the death will be waged tomorrow.
One which you intend to win because you have the most
guns."

Bonano couldn't resist smiling. "And all over you,
Major. All this trouble, all this killing over one man. Don't
you feel important?"

"I feel like kicking your ass."

Bonano chuckled. He was liking the major more by the
minute.

"Major, I will return you to your cell, under heavy
guard. Get some sleep, Major. Tomorrow, it promises to be
a big day. *Buenas noches.*"

The guards hauled Major Ellis out of the room.

Once again, Bonano opened the money trunk. He
crouched, picked up a stack of bills, and riffled their clean,
crisp edges. He liked the feel of American money in his
hands. It made him feel powerful, alive. He was Attila,
after all, the most feared Hun in all of Central America. He
had been given complete charge and control of the zone by
the army, and he answered to no man. No man.

Tomorrow, he thought, would prove most interesting.
And after tomorrow, once his men had wiped out the CIA
assassins and he had hung the heads of *El Tigre* and the four
mercenaries from the front wall of the garrison, he would
turn the major over to Kubchkin.

Tomorrow, many wrongs would be made right. He intended to put Nicaragua on the world map, and he, Attila the Hun, would be known and feared throughout all the Western Hemisphere.

Miguel Horchiba Bonano didn't think he would be able to sleep.

Chapter 11

Two flares, jammed into the soft earth of the jungle clearing, sparked and crackled to life. Vic Gabriel walked away from the wharf, found himself face-to-face with an enormously fat man. Grinning, the fat man stuck a huge cigar in his piggish sweaty face. He had one of his six cronies fire up the stogie with a Zippo and said to the guy, "'Preciate that, soldier."

M16 low by his side, Gabriel took several more steps into the wavering circle of light. He already knew what he was faced with—trouble he didn't need.

"Okay, partner," the fat man began. "Let's get down to business here. I'm Colonel Hank Tilton. U.S. Army. Retired. You could say I'm a free-lancer, kinda like yourself. I got my own small army, just like you. Crack. All of 'em. Best around."

"Stuff the flattery, fat man, and get on with it."

"Touchy, ain't we? A little too big for your britches to be talking to a man who's got your lovely little señorita."

"What do you want?"

"Simple. It's like this. I ain't gonna bullshit ya, and I ain't gonna repeat myself, so listen up good. All of *El Tigre's* studs have been castrated back there. Now . . . just to show you I mean business and just to show you I ain't partial about who or what I kill to get what I want . . . Jocko!"

Gabriel watched with mounting rage and fear. He saw the two struggling shadows behind the fat man. Lolita? No. He heard the voice of fear echo out of the jungle, a familiar voice.

"No . . . no . . . you can't . . . no . . . please . . . don't . . ."

Gabriel recognized the Hippie's voice. He saw the merc called Jocko thrust Hippie to his knees and lift the machete over his head.

"Nooooooo!"

A dull but loud thunk.

The shadow tossed the Hippie's severed head into the ring of light. The head rolled up at Gabriel's feet and dead eyes stared accusingly up at the ex–Special Forces warrior. No matter what he had been, the Hippie, Gabriel thought, still didn't deserve to die that way. Nor did *El Tigre*'s men deserve to be butchered and left as a bloody meal for the scavengers of the jungle.

"There's my peace offering, tough guy," Tilton went on, chomping on his cigar. "Now, I'm proposing this. Banana is sitting on a cool million he took from that CIA armada he blew out of the sky. I want the money. That simple. Me and my boys will team up with you and go headhunt for this Banana Man at his garrison. We're both hunting the same spic son of a bitch, so I figure let's be buddies for the duration, all right. Let's see here . . . looks like we'll have about thirty guns between us. Won't be easy, but it'll make that cool million that much sweeter."

"And if I say no, you kill the woman?"

Tilton blew smoke, the grin fixed on his fat face. "You're a smart one, I like that. I think we can do business together."

"That's it, huh. I just let you and your people tag along for the raid. You find the million, walk away with it, and I'm supposed to trust you to give me back the woman. Alive and unharmed."

"You got a choice?"

"Doesn't seem like it."

"Now, I know what you're thinking. How in the world are you gonna trust me and my boys to keep from cutting you and your boys down once the raid is over? Answer. You can't. But like you said, son—"

"And what if you don't make it back to San Pedro?"

Tilton hitched up his pants. "Good question. We get on

those gunboats you so kindly provided for us and hit the garrison before sunup. Get in, get out, kill anything and everything that moves, I don't give a shit what it is. Nicaraguan. American soldiers. CIA. The pope, I don't give a shit. I want that money, and it's ours. You don't get nothin' but the woman back and the satisfaction of knowing that money is rightfully back in the hands of Uncle's finest. Now . . . I've already cleared out San Pee-dro. Ain't a living soul there, not even a fucking dog pissing in the bushes. The woman, she's been taken back there by two of my best. They're gonna sit on her, so to speak. Don't worry, they won't lay a hand on her, they already shot their wad on them nuns back at San Pee-dro."

Tilton chuckled and several of his men also joined in his sick humor.

Gabriel felt an iceball of rage lodge in his guts, sensed the murderous fury of *El Tigre* behind him as the Contra rebel leader quietly, viciously cursed Tilton and swore to himself that the fat man would pay.

"Vic," Henry van Boolewarke quietly called out. "I know what you're going to do, old man."

"He's right," Johnny Simms added. "I say we throw down on this cracker motherfucker right here. How do we know she isn't already dead?"

"Don't be stupid, nigger boy." Tilton laughed. "Tough guy here don't wanna be wastin' a fine piece of ass like Lolita."

Defiant hatred glowed in the eyes of the black merc, but he held his ground in silence, his jaw clenching like two pieces of meshing machinery. Gabriel could feel Simms tense up behind him, a breath or a word away from opening up with his M16 on the fat man.

"Do what you gotta do, VG," Bad Zac Dillinger said. "This fat fuck has got us bent over a barrel. 'Sides, we could use the extra firepower now."

"Now there's a thinking man's man," Tilton said, gloating. "I like you, son. What's your name?"

"Death. Disemboweler of fat ex-colonels."

Tilton laughed. "Boy, oh, boy, I love it. A funny man's funny man, too. Okay. Back to your original question.

You'll have to take my word about the woman. Now . . . I don't make it back to San Pee-dro tomorrow by high noon, my boys have already been given permission to do what they want with your woman. And I gotta tell ya they'll have gotten a good night's sleep." Tilton casually kicked the Hippie's head aside, stepped up, and blew smoke in Gabriel's face. "They'll probably hit sunup with a coupla mean piss hard-ons . . . y'know, the kind that just won't go away unless you do somethin' about it. . . ."

His hand snaking out, Gabriel grabbed Tilton by the throat. Tilton almost gagged on his cigar, but the stogie fell from his open mouth, his eyes bulging as he was forced to his knees.

Both sides tensed, leveling weapons at each other. As if sensing the situation primed to explode, hundreds of bats suddenly took the air above the canopy, flapping and screeching at the night, diving and fluttering around in wild circles over the tree line.

"Don't . . . shoot . . ." Tilton croaked.

The most terrible rage he had ever felt consumed Vic Gabriel. His burning stare nearly hidden by hooded eyelids, he trembled with fury, desiring only to crush the life out of the fat man.

"If that woman is harmed, if you've killed her . . . or kill her . . ."

"Easy . . . you're choking me. . . ."

Gabriel flung the fat man to the ground, his chest heaving with a volcanic fury set to erupt into insanity. He pulled himself back from that edge of madness. A collective breath had been trapped in the lungs of Eagle Force and *El Tigre* and his Contras and Tilton's mercs. One loud pent-up breath seemed expelled as one.

As Gabriel wheeled and began walking away from Tilton, he growled back, "Get your fat ass on that boat. Before I change my mind and nobody walks out of here alive."

Major Ivan Kubchkin had already gotten word about the slaughter at San Pedro by his recon patrol. He had also gotten a grim update from Bonano at the garrison.

The plan was set.

A major battle was forthcoming.

Kubchkin led twenty of his commandos and twenty more Sandinistas through the jungle. They stuck to the main trail, knowing the enemy was well ahead of them, moving for the river. They wanted the gunboats, and it was as safe and sure a plan of attack as any, Kubchkin knew. The river was not well patrolled. It should have been, and Kubchkin had warned Bonano about that months ago. Kubchkin mentally added up Bonano's score. Bonano came out with a zero, and as a zero. There were going to be some changes after the battle, the SPETSNAZ major decided.

And Kubchkin was eagerly anticipating the fight.

It would be a classic pincer assault. Kubchkin had approved Bonano's plan. Let the strike force storm the garrison. Allow them inside while offering almost token resistance. Kubchkin and his unit would move in from behind. There was a chance the garrison would be leveled, but he would take that chance. There was also the chance the four mercenaries, whoever they were, would die during the battle. That was fine with Kubchkin. As long as Major Ellis was finally handed over to him, very little else mattered.

Then there was the report of the CIA hit team, on its way to the zone. That was to be expected, Kubchkin thought. The American military advisers responsible for bringing the arms shipment to Nicaragua had failed, and the CIA, who had financed the covert operation, couldn't afford to have the operation made world knowledge.

AK47 in hand, Kubchkin followed closely behind the point men. He scoured the jungle. *Chort vozmi!* The howler monkeys and insect noise made it impossible to hear any movement around them. He had to know what was out there at all times, so he had sent recon patrols ahead. They had found something, just moments ago. Another slaughter. Contras had been stabbed, had their throats cut, or had been shot dead by somebody . . . Who? There were reports that a renegade U.S. Army colonel was in the zone with a pack of his own mercenaries, but those reports had not been confirmed.

The situation was about to reach critical mass, Kubchkin knew.

Then he heard it, and ordered the column to stop. To a man, they crouched off to the side of the trail. It was the familiar whapping bleat of rotor blades that made Kubchkin look up. He spotted the gunships. Two of them. American gunships, Hueys. They soared low over the jungle canopy, and Kubchkin felt the rotor wash slapping against his sweaty face as the tree line wavered for a moment in the slipstream of the gunships. Then they were gone.

"Ivyask!" Kubchkin called out to one of his point men. "Take a squad with you. Find that gunship. Report back. Be quick about it."

"*Da*, Comrade Major."

Ivask gathered a dozen Sandinistas and they melted into the jungle.

"Move out!" Kubchkin barked.

As the column began wending its way down the trail, he thought about those gunships, but he knew already who, or rather what, was aboard those choppers. The CIA assassin team.

Very well, Major Ivan Kubchkin decided. It only meant that Bonano's garrison would become a boneyard for still more *Amerikanski*. And better still, he thought, perhaps Bonano would not live to see the sunrise himself.

It was time for fresh blood, new leadership in the zone anyway. Someone Kubchkin could more easily control. Bonano was as much a renegade as the men he would lure to their deaths. Kubchkin had no room for individuals, no tolerance for renegades who would act on their own.

Ivan Kubchkin would control the zone, or he knew he wouldn't make it back to Little Mother Russia alive. Moscow would not permit it.

The Iceman hopped out of the gunship fuselage. He was ready to go, but knew he had to be patient. Patience and timing were keys to an assassin's success. Planning and execution the soldier's best friends. He considered himself both assassin and soldier. He was the best. Which was why he had been hired in the first place, and damn the CIA anyway.

He was determined to survive to collect his money from the bastards at Langley.

Dawn was still a few hours away, but Iceman knew he would head out before the first crack of light spilled over the jungle. Had to. During the stage of an operation like this, the worst thing to do is to sit still, he had always believed. Movement and action created luck, and motion relieved pent-up tension. He knew all of them would need a little bit of good fortune if they were to make it out of Nicaragua alive. He knew there would be casualties, dead men left behind. And he was certain the CIA was hoping none of them would make it out alive. That was just the way they did business. They had fucked up and were now hoping to wipe the slate clean, wash their hands of this dirty business. They had dipped into the cesspool and gotten shit smeared all over them. They had made the big attempt to make the big score with the Contras, but had their candy snatched away from them by the big bad bullyboys, the Sandinistas. Fuck 'em, Iceman thought. Fuck everybody. He was primed. Set to waste anything that got in his way.

As his men and his gunship pilots gathered around him, he prepared to give them the final brief. It would be short, as usual, and to the brutal point. His men were nameless as far as he was concerned, so he numbered them, one through twelve. He didn't even want to know their names. It was best not to get personal.

Rotor blades on both gunships slowly spun to a stop. They were gathered behind the gunships at the edge of the clearing. Darkness engulfed them, but every man wore infrared goggles. Iceman removed his goggles, adjusted his sight to the darkness.

"Listen up, this is it."

He was impressed with their armament. M16s with M203 grenade launchers. M60 machine guns, belted and ready to rip. LAWs rocket launchers. Uzi subguns. A two-man team with automatic grenade launchers. Ka-Bars and grenades and dozens of spare ammo clips. The stage was set. He was pumped up on adrenaline, eager to kick ass, and he knew they were chomping at the bit.

"We take both gunships in," Iceman said. "We hit the target area, hard. One team disembark inside, the other on the outside. We level their goddamn house. I want a rocket team with me all the way in and out. I know what Ellis looks like, I seen him before. But we're icing everything inside that garrison that breathes. Everything. Nothing but us walks out of there alive, people.

"Now, in the event we lose the gunships, an emergency exfiltration team is on standby to pull us out. Don't count on them. Count on yourselves. We have to march through the jungle all the way into Honduras with the Sandinistas right on our asses, that's what we'll do. All right, you got thirty minutes to check your weapons, look inside yourselves, and dig it out. Lock and load, people. This is it."

And it was, he knew.

Some of them weren't going home.

Maybe nobody was going back.

Chapter 12

From the bow of the gunboat, Vic Gabriel stared down the river, peering into the darkness. The darkness was impenetrable. But when he looked inside, he found that darkness overwhelming, threatening to suffocate him with a burden he had never before known. He had serious problems, seemingly insurmountable problems on his hands. If it was physically possible, he would have kicked himself in the ass. His heart ached for Lolita. He had sent her back and put her life on the line, that was even if she was still alive. If the fat man had killed her, the fat man would die. He would see to it himself.

He checked the other gunboat off to the port. Both gunboats were sliding through the dark waters at fifteen knots.

Destination: Hell.

Like always, no matter how bad things got, Vic Gabriel would deal with the situation. There was never any other way, was there? To run, to hide, to duck, to look for an easy alternative is to die. It is that way with anything in life. Searching for the easy way had never been Vic Gabriel's way. You took a stand, you stood up, and if you took some lumps, then that's just the way it is. Get knocked on your ass, get back up. To do less is to die. Both physically and spiritually. Often, the hard way is frowned upon by some-one looking in from the outside, Vic Gabriel reflected, but the hard way is the best way, the only way. It builds the foundation of a man's character. It tests him. It drives him. It allows him to see himself and the world as it is, for what it is. Sometimes, though, the hard way can backfire and it can all come crumbling down around you. But even in this there is a freedom of will, because you tested yourself, did it your way, and learned from whatever mistake was made. The next time out, you will be stronger and more prepared.

Vic Gabriel liked it the hard way. And if he was to die in Nicaragua, then he was determined to die like he had lived. The hard way.

As part of the plan of the advance with his unholy alliance with Tilton, Gabriel had his team split up between the gunboats. Simms and Dillinger were aboard the other gunboat, with Tilton's cutthroats manning the .50-caliber machine guns, stern and bow. Dutch was with Gabriel, and now the Afrikaaner quietly moved up behind the ex–Special Forces warrior. Dutch, Barnett Panzer crossbow slung around his shoulder, the M60 leaning up against a bench within easy reach, wore a grim and heavy look.

"I would have done the same thing, old man. Don't beat yourself up. We need you to pull us through. She needs you."

Turning, Gabriel checked the stern. As prearranged with Tilton, *El Tigre*'s men John Wayne and Zorro stood ready in the .50-caliber machine-gun turrets, prepared to cut down the Fat Man and his mercs at the first hint of a double cross. Gabriel spotted the Fat Man standing in the stern, puffing on a cigar, gazing out at the river. The ex–Special Forces warrior imagined the glowing cigar tip as a bull's-eye.

There would be time later, though, for vengeance. He hoped.

Gabriel had been assured by *El Tigre* that there were no more Sandinistas in the immediate area, no more gunboat checkpoints. They would find out. They would find out a number of things. They would find all these things out the hard way.

Gabriel spat over the side. "You know how it is, so I don't need to say a whole lot. I'm torn between two worlds, and I'm trying to save both of them, pull it all back in."

"This, uh, this Major Ellis," Dutch said, showing Gabriel a warm smile. "He must be worth it."

"He is. He's one of us."

And Vic Gabriel just stared off into the night. His own words seemed to echo through his head, and called him back into an abyss of tortured memories.

He is. He's one of us.

It seemed to take a hundred years for Vic Gabriel to pry his eyelids open. The world was hazy, faded in and out, and he tried to focus on some point of light, but there was no light, at least not at first. He was floating on a cloud, knew he'd been doped up on a healthy shot of morphine. He was numb, and there was no pain. He felt good, and he wanted to stay there forever on that drifting painless cloud. It would be hard to go back.

But he couldn't stay where he was, or they would have won in the end. He knew he was alive and life would bring him back to the grim present. He was a soldier, a warrior, and suddenly he felt as if there were some larger purpose to his life, some purpose he wasn't sure of yet, but something that he was meant to do and he couldn't die or be killed until he had done it. He was wounded, he knew, and wasn't sure how seriously he was hurt. But he was alive. Something deep inside told him that he had been meant to live all along. In a way, it was a frightening feeling, to walk away from the icy touch of death and survive and be faced with your own mortality. It can put you in a very scary and very lonely place. It makes you more aware than ever before that someday it will happen and there won't be a damn thing you can do about it.

As he tried to focus his vision, he found he was surrounded by a wall of black. Then, as reality slowly clawed its way in, he realized he was lying on a bed, and a partition sealed off the area around him. There were tubes stuck in his arm, and he was wrapped up in bandages, damn near from head to toe.

It was all starting to come back to him. The Buddhist temple. The Cong charge. The bullets tearing into his body. The blood spraying over his face.

The gunship.

The face. He began to see him then. As the white fog slowly parted, he saw and recognized that grizzled face hovering over him. The guy who had hauled his bullet-riddled ass out of no-man's-land. His savior.

"Wh-what . . ."

"Easy, son. You're safe now. You're still Vic Gabriel, and I'm still Captain Ben Ellis. You're in my own personal quarters, complete with a good-looking nurse and enough painkillers to take you to Mars, if that's where you'd like to go."

He tried to sit up, groaned.

"Suggest you don't move, son. You ate enough Cong lead to drop a rhino, and you got more bandages wrapped around you than King Tut. Some people would say you're damn lucky to be alive. I call it something else."

"Yeah. Like what, Captain? What am I if I'm not lucky?"

"I spent some time down in Mexico a while back. They got a saying down there. It fits where you are and even more importantly what you are. The Mexicans, they say the mad are touched by the gods."

Young Vic Gabriel didn't know if he liked that. "You think I'm crazy?"

"Not crazy like you might think. You got what I call the look about you. I like to call it an aura. I've seen it before on soldiers, like to think maybe that aura protects me. Any number of those slugs going through you a fraction of an inch any other way would've killed you, but they didn't. A lesser man would have just died from the loss of blood, or maybe despaired and just given up. But you got the Look, and you got that Look inside you. That's what kept you alive. It goes a lot further and a lot deeper than just the will to survive."

Gabriel tried a weak smile. It hurt his face. "You saying somebody somewhere's looking out for me."

Ellis pulled up a chair, torched up a cigar with a Zippo. "Something like that. It can't really be explained, but some men just have it. It wasn't your time, and it won't be your time for a long, long time. You got a lot of wars ahead of you. You aren't going to die in this bullshit mess called a war because you're not meant to. I can see it. I almost wouldn't want to be you for nothing. The rest of *your life might seem like an eternity, and you'll be torn and tugged back and forth between the light and the dark. You just got it, son, deal with it. One of the things about it is that you got a way of living for the moment and in the moment. Most of us do one or the other, or neither."*

Gabriel peered closely at Ellis. The man was dressed in black, sported only a .45 Colt on his hip. Ellis didn't act or look like standard by-the-book government issue. Despite the strange way he talked, Gabriel could tell the guy was dead serious, even though there was a sardonic glint in his eyes, as if he was debating with himself whether or not to share his private little joke on the world with you. The way he talked, hinting at and digging for some deeper meaning to the insanity of the world, he could have been a mirror image of Gabriel's father. But just what the hell was he saying anyway? The Look? Touched by the gods? A lifetime that would seem like an eternity? Was the captain trying to say he was blessed somehow, to go through a life of pain and suffering and close brushes with death, and meant to endure it all? Was that a blessing? Or was it a curse? If that was the case, young Vic Gabriel wasn't sure he wanted any part of a life like that.

A wry smile danced over his lips. "You got a crystal ball somewhere in here, Captain?"

Ellis puffed on his stogie, grinned. "I got the Eyes, son. I've seen enough to be able to separate the winners from the losers."

Gabriel didn't want to think about the Look anymore. He abruptly changed the subject. "Do you know what happened back there? What went wrong?"

"I know what I saw. All the men in your squad were killed, through no fault of your own. You were set up. That's what I hear."

"By who?"

"I think we both know who. Saunders."

"How do you know about Saunders?"

"I know this. You and your father, the highly respected Colonel Charles Gabriel, have got your own special father-and-son behind-the-lines team. I've heard you two are damn good together, the best in this man's army. Your *father's become something of an institution over here. About the only thing they don't do when they talk about him is bless themselves. I know about you and your father because I got my own Special Operations Unit within the 101st. I got connections, I see things, remember. I got the Eyes.*

"It's no big secret that Saunders and some of his people are running opium and guns over here. It's a big Company scam, but nobody can or will touch them. Haven't you heard, son? It's all a battle of bullshit. Your blood, their profit. Doesn't mean you quit and walk away. This is your honing ground, son. This is where you start to become what I know you will become."

"And what's that?"

A ghost of a smile danced over the captain's lips. "A savior . . . of sorts. A warrior, definitely."

"Yeah. The eternal life of pain and suffering and close calls with death, right. A savior, huh, a warrior, huh, fighting for the little man." Young Vic Gabriel almost wanted to laugh at the thought of himself as some kind of hero. It was a role he didn't think he would want under any circumstances. A guy becomes a hero, an example of good and righteous living and all that crap, he thought, and the fall is a lot longer, a lot harder, and a lot more brutal and final. The kind of fall that could lock a man in that scary lonely place forever. Hell, it would be a lonely, scary place to begin with, but somebody's gotta do it, right? the young soldier joked to himself. "Like Superman, doing battle against the bad guys and saving the world?"

"Something like that."

Gabriel realized Ellis had managed to change his line of thought, so he abruptly got back on track. "Tell me about Saunders. What do you know?"

Ellis shrugged, blew some smoke. "Not much, unfortunately, not anything anybody can prove. But that's the CIA, and nothing with those guys will ever change, and maybe it's not meant to be any different. They cover their asses good and they get themselves hooked up with the top brass, and we, the little people, are expected to see no evil and like that."

"So, that's it."

"That's it. Nobody knows of or has heard about your mission, officially that is. Cambodia's off limits, soldier, everybody knows that. But you knew the deal. It stinks, yeah, that the wheels in the machinery keep grinding on and Saunders and his Company goons fatten their wallets and you lay there fighting for your next breath."

"Why? Why did it go down the way it did?"

"It's pretty obvious from what I could gather. I imagine Saunders figured you or your father or both had something on him. Classic setup for termination with extreme prejudice and all that. The CIA set your operation up and sent you out there, at Saunders's bequest, understand. Got word to the Cong about the why, when, where, and how. A nice neat little ambush package gift-wrapped and handed to them. Saunders must be running a little scared to take the chance of killing those soldiers just to get you. He's playing God, and right now nobody can touch him. Saunders playing God made me angry enough to butt myself in and go out and get you."

A bitter taste of bile rolled up in Gabriel's mouth. He just stared ahead for several moments. It stunk, all right. But what was he going to do anyway? Nobody had really proven a thing against Saunders. Yet. And if they did, who would do what? Who really even cared? Did that make him and every foot soldier over there nothing more than cannon fodder to be used and discarded in order to keep the big wheels on the machinery rolling right along. It didn't make a damn bit of sense.

But something did make sense, and it had been proven by the man who had saved his life. Something that made sense out of all this madness. And young Vic Gabriel was not about to let it go unacknowledged.

"Captain."

Ellis looked deep into Gabriel's eyes, puffed on his cigar.

"I owe you."

A strange smile cut the captain's lips, made him seem years older than he was. "I know. And I know that you know that. I don't expect you to, but someday I know you'll

*square it. Stay alive, soldier. That'll be thanks enough for
this old man."*

"Wake up, son. Stop jerking yourself off there."

Gabriel spun, hauled out of his thoughts by the grating
voice of the Fat Man. His eyes blazing with anger, he
leveled his stare on Tilton. The Fat Man just stood there
behind him, puffing contentedly on his cigar. That cigar was
looking like a bigger and fatter bull's-eye by the minute.

"Got no time to be daydreaming, boy. We're there."

Gabriel was vaguely aware of Dutch standing next to
him, aware, too, that *El Tigre* was there beside him.

"Hombre," *El Tigre* said to Gabriel. "We are less than
three kilometers from the garrison."

"All right, a little further, then pull it over. We walk it
in."

El Tigre nodded, cast Tilton one final baleful look, then
returned to his men.

Gabriel looked Tilton dead in the eye. "I'm going to
tell you something, Fat Man. You can do just about
whatever you want when we hit that garrison, but there's
somebody there, an American, I'm here to pull out. Don't
let him get killed. If he even gets scratched up, I'll be
looking for you."

Gabriel stepped past Tilton, but the Fat Man said, "No
sweat, son. you do what you gotta do, I do my thing. Just
so long as I get that million, understand?"

Turning, Gabriel held his ground for a long moment. A
strange smile cut his lips. "Don't count that money yet, Fat
Man."

"Yeah. What's that supposed to mean?"

Gabriel pointed his hand at Tilton like he would hold
a gun.

"It means," the ex–Special Forces warrior said, grim,
tight-lipped, as he dropped his thumb, "that I might start
looking real hard at that cigar jammed in your face. And if
you see the Look in my eye, you'll know you've overdrawn
your account."

Gabriel and Dutch left Tilton standing alone, scowling
and muttering to himself.

Chapter 13

He had thought about the possibility of disaster, and in case it didn't go his way Miguel Horchiba Bonano had an insurance plan. At the moment, he was working out his insurance, making certain his men set the fifty-five-gallon gasoline drums in the right place.

Dawn was less than an hour away, and suddenly Bonano was becoming nervous. The sentries along the ramparts had not seen or heard a thing out there in the jungle, except the ever-present and damnable howler monkeys. He had ordered all lights along the ramparts doused, and his men to survey the jungle through infrared binoculars. Two klieg lights bathed the courtyard, and Bonano sensed the tension of his men as they patrolled the gloom. They paced the ramparts and courtyard like caged lions. Other soldiers manned .50-caliber machine guns, secured inside sandbags. Like some great oppressive weight, a terrible silence hung over the garrison. Bonano was beginning to wonder if he was doing the right thing by letting the invaders come to him. But there was no other way, was there? To go out into the jungle and hunt the enemy on their terms would be suicide. At least at the garrison he could watch and monitor and call the action.

Bonano stood at the top of the steps leading into the cellblock. The lids on the twelve drums had been removed, as he had ordered. In the event he was faced with an uncontrollable situation, he would dangle the lives of the surviving eighteen American military advisers, including Captain Ellis, over the heads of the invaders. He would let them decide the fate of their own people.

Bonano moved halfway down the steps, peering into the flickering torchlight. His men quickly set the empty wine bottles beside each and every cell. Gasoline-soaked rags were crammed into the necks of the bottles. If he was forced to set the cellblock ablaze, it would be a horrible thing to watch and listen to the prisoners being burned alive, but he had no choice.

The invaders were coming.

Coming to take the zone away from him.

Coming to clean up their own mess.

"Everything in order?" Bonano called and heard, "*Sí, Comandante,*" echoed back at him from the bowels of the cellblock.

If either one of them were to die now, the dream, too, would die and all would be lost. Lolita Armandez had a tough decision to make. But she had already made that decision before her captors had marched into the slaughterzone that was San Pedro.

They had tossed her in the church and let her just lie among the rubble, smelling the death all around her, staring at the massacre and wondering just what it was that made men do this kind of thing. Lolita Armandez hated these two men. They were like animals. No, they were less than animals, not even as good as animals. They had been part of the Fat Man's force that had slaughtered everyone in San Pedro. There had been no reason, no reason at all to do such a thing. But animals don't reason, she told herself, they live on sheer brute instinct. Not even the brute and savage predators of the animal kingdom murdered their own. Only man did that.

Rage, grief, fear tore through her. What of Gabriel? Was he still alive? If he was, then she had no doubt he would come back for her. Between now and then, what would she do? What could she do?

The two who called themselves Pac Man and Wilco sat on the rubble near her, sipping from wine bottles they had scavenged from the ruins. They smoked cigarettes and looked at her, their eyes burning with lust. They fondled themselves and talked about what they would do to her.

They kept their M16s within easy reach and spoke of obscene things they would like to do to her using their assault rifles. But they seemed afraid of her, and she found that amusing. Two big tough mercenaries, thumping their chests in arrogant pride and talking big and tough, afraid, it seemed, of one lone woman. But isn't it always the ones, she thought, who talk the loudest, who brag the most, who always turn out to be without backbone?

She felt the sharp edge of a stone digging into the ropes that bound her hands. She kept an eye on them, and began rubbing the ropes against the stone. She would free herself. She would lure one of them to her, then take his knife and kill him, take his M16, and shoot the other one. She had to. There was no other way. The thought of what could happen if she did nothing terrified her.

She was too close now to let the dream slip away.

"Ah, my little chiquita banana, I want to peel you back and spread you wide," the one called Wilco said, laughing, and slurped some wine from the bottle. "Y'know, babes, I almost hope the Fat Man doesn't make it back. He said we could do what we wanted with you if he didn't make it back by noon."

Pac Man looked at his Rolex. "And I'm counting the minutes, baby cakes, I'll tell ya that. Heh-heh. I think I got quarter till right now." He laughed, too. "No, sorry, I guess I set my watch up by mistake. But me and you, I think we were meant for each other. What do you say?"

There. The stone had sliced through the ropes.

She looked at each man in turn and forced herself to smile. She had to do it now. While they were on the verge of drinking themselves into a stupor. They would rape her anyway. And they would probably kill her after, not even thinking about how they would have to answer to the Fat Man. Or to Gabriel.

"I say . . . you are going to do it anyway . . . so why not get it over with. Come here then and do it. If you are a man."

They looked at each other, confused, it seemed, for a moment.

"Well, how 'bout this, Wilco? What do you think?"

Wilco chuckled. "I think we got some time to kill before noon. And I think there's more man here than she can handle."

They both laughed, chugging wine.

"Flip for it," Wilco said.

Pac Man tossed a coin into the air, called, "Heads."

Wilco won the toss. Pac Man muttered a curse.

"Okay, babes," she heard the animal say, and move toward her. "Let's get it on."

As he reached for her, his lips slobbering and his eyes mad with lust, Lolita lunged for his sheathed commando dagger and pulled the blade free.

"All right, now that we're here, now what? Tell me that, smart guy. Now that you're lookin' at it, what's the deal here?"

"Keep your goddamn voice down," Vic Gabriel rasped at the Fat Man.

Tilton looked amused. Gabriel was anything but amused.

"You're the big army colonel, Uncle Sam's finest," Bad Zac Dillinger growled, "you tell us."

Tilton looked out across the short stretch of no-man's-land, his fat face furrowed in thought.

Flanked by his commandos, Gabriel took in the scene, too. The total combined strike force was crouched at the edge of the jungle tree line. The jungle was almost right on top of the garrison. It could have been any one of countless Spanish forts scattered all up and down the lower Americas. Maybe thirty meters separated the jungle from the garrison. The first smudge of dirty gray light had streaked across the sky. They were right on schedule, Gabriel decided, but it was going to be anything but easy to get inside the garrison.

A fifteen-foot-high stone wall ran a good hundred meters along the front and a huge wooden gate sat dead center in the front wall. *El Tigre* had already given Gabriel the layout. Roughly rectangular, the garrison had to be big if it took up nearly as much space as the village of San Pedro. Gabriel could see the dark shadows marching along the ramparts behind the wall. He counted a dozen heads. It was strange, he thought, that they had encountered nothing in the form of sentries outside the garrison, hardened up at attention to ring a defensive perimeter around the fort. Perhaps they were expected, Gabriel thought, and decided that was the only thing that really made any sense. No resistance. No patrols in the jungle. Attila the Hun had a plan. There was only one way to uncover that plan.

Tilton checked his troops, looked at *El Tigre* and his men, and said, "Okay, it's like this, since you seem to need my expert opinion so much. I'll do my best to try and walk you boys through it."

"Big of you," Simms said, then muttered to Dillinger, "How the hell does somethin' like that make colonel in the U.S. Army?"

Dillinger shrugged, spat. "Same way a dopehead can run an entire major city. They bullshit their way in and you don't realize what you got until you're stuck with it."

If Tilton heard them, he chose to ignore the barbs. "We got plenty of rocket firepower here, and I don't see no hope of any fleet of F16s flying in to soften up the target with a nice big air strike. Spread some of these troops out on all points around the target. Open up the same time with the rockets and make a run at 'em. Take out as many as you can with first big blows and then everybody's on their own."

"*El Tigre*," Gabriel said. "Any other gates into hell?"

The Contra rebel leader nodded. "*Sí*. At the south and east ends. Same size. Big enough to get transport trucks through without a problem."

"Okay, *El Tigre*, check your watch for ten minutes, get in position, and unload those rocket launchers on the gates and the walls. There's no easy way in. Hit first and hit hard. Good luck."

Gabriel checked his watch, then he heard it. A strange sound, but a familiar one. He looked toward the sky and the whapping bleat began to loom larger, louder to the north, directly behind them.

Bonano heard it, too. He looked up at the dirty gray jungle sky. He felt a tremor of fear, and knew they had arrived. He walked away from his command HQ. He turned and looked at the men he had ordered to secure his contingency plan. They were crouched on the stairwell leading into the cellblock, ready to kick the drums over at his order.

High above the jungle tree line, he saw them. Two of them. Black against black, swooping low and coming in at the garrison in a strafing run, like two giant predatory birds.

Suddenly his men were scrambling along the ramparts, crouching, aiming their AK47s skyward.

Iceman gave the order.

"Let it rip!"

Rocket pods flamed and miniguns unleashed a thunderous hellrain of lead.

Standing in the fuselage doorway, half of his nameless dozen right behind him, armed to the teeth, the Iceman watched as the gunships swooped low toward the garrison. The courtyard was the destination. Set it down. Disembark the guns and chew it up.

A line of explosions peppered the front wall of the garrison. Bodies took the sky on raging tongues of fire.

The Iceman was locked and loaded.

"Who the bloody hell are these guys!?" Dutch yelled.

They were all looking toward the sky as the gunships streaked overhead and zeroed in on the garrison, nose down and spitting fire and lead, hellbirds of prey.

"U.S. Army or CIA?" Simms rasped as explosions puked gaping holes in the front wall of the garrison and men screamed and flew through the air, bloody broken hunks of savaged meat.

"Or both?" Boolewarke added.

Gabriel didn't know, but he sure as hell cared. If they were U.S. troops he didn't need their blood on his hands. But if they were U.S. soldiers or even CIA, there was only one reason why they were there. Exfiltrate or terminate their own. Only one way to go, one way to find out which it was.

"Goddammit!" Tilton roared. "Those bastards are

gonna fuck everything up! They're gonna fuck my money up all to hell! Goddamnit! Goddammit!"

"Don't fire on them unless they fire on you!" Gabriel ordered.

"Fuck that, boy! I got a big investment in this thing!"

Gabriel ignored Tilton, setting his sights on bigger and more savage game.

Balls of fire boiled down the front of the garrison wall. The gunships punched into the blossoming clouds of smoke and fire and disappeared.

"Let's hit it!" Gabriel bellowed, broke from cover, and led the charge across no-man's-land.

And *El Tigre* and his rebels cut loose with massive rocket firepower.

Vic Gabriel checked the illuminated dial of his Seiko. It was five minutes till midnight. It was agonizing to have to wait all those silent hours for the shelling to begin to hit the town. But come it would. Any second. There was no option for the three of them but to wait it out and take it all as it came down, Gabriel knew. The worst thing they could do would be to go off into the jungle and engage the enemy on their terms, on dark and unfamiliar turf. Out in the open, they stood a fighting chance. A slim one. Gabriel was certain Saunders would soften up the town first with a massive mortar bombardment, then move right in for what he hoped would be an easy mop-up detail.

Three tall shadows, Gabriel, Dillinger, and Simms strolled down the middle of the street, checking the jungle and dark blocks of buildings with grim and wary gazes. Belted M60 cradled by Simms, M16s for Gabriel and Dillinger, locked and loaded. The darkness was total, and the silence, except for the shriek of howler monkeys and the eternal buzz of insects from the surrounding black bastions of jungle, was oppressive. A burro brayed from somewhere in the night, and Gabriel, combat senses on full alert, spotted the scavenger dogs roaming wild in the streets, waiting for the blood to run hot so they could sniff out a feast of flesh.

"What's the name of this place anyway, VG?" Dillinger asked. "Least like to know where I'm going to be buried."

"I don't know," Gabriel answered. "Never heard it called anything. As for being buried, if you die here, the wild dogs will take care of that. They'll pick you clean. Everything down here feeds on death. It's like one great long conveyor belt of death that feeds and nourishes the life cycle."

"Great," Simms gruffed. "Here we are, three mercenary Gary Coopers, in a town with no name, and a blind woman prophet who sees only death. And the witching hour is almost upon us. I seen it all now."

"Well, look at it like this, Johnny boy," Dillinger said, "you die here, you won't owe anybody any money back home. You can take all your debt to the grave with you."

"I think I'm feeling better already," Simms cracked with a mean smile. "I knew there was an answer to all my problems somewhere. Looks like I'm gonna hit bingo in a jungle border town in Nicaragua. Thank you, Lord, for looking out for this poor black soul."

At precisely midnight, as Gabriel had anticipated, the shelling began. As planned, they split off, seeking cover in the nooks and crevices of buildings. The sound of mortars whistling through the air instantly became one endless carumphing din. A line of explosions ripped through the buildings on both sides of the street. Fireballs razored huge sheets of rubble and metal through the air. Smoke boiled and flames meshed into one long wavering wall of fire.

Gabriel hit the steps of what he assumed was some kind of hotel. Welcome to the Hotel Nicaragua, he sardonically thought as the roar of explosions tore through his brain and shattered his senses. He burst into the empty lobby as the planks behind him erupted in a roiling bed of fire. Shock waves hurled him to the ground. Through the fury of the mortar barrage, he made out the rotor wash. Growing. Looming.

The gunship, he knew, carrying Saunders.

Then another series of explosions tore the night asunder. Flashes of fire showed beyond the windows and doorway. Walls of dust cycloned into the firestorm as the gunship streaked low down the street. It disappeared from Gabriel's sight, then came back, unloading another rocket payload on the buildings. The earth shook beneath Gabriel as the concussive bomb-blasts peppered their way toward his position—not so much what he heard, but what he felt. As if the earth was about to open up and swallow him whole.

Gabriel dived through a window, shielding his face with his M16, as the expected tornado of fireballs uprooted the Hotel Nicaragua. Glass chips raining down around him, he hit the planks, looked up. Shards of woods and debris pounded the street in front of Gabriel and smoke and dust hazed the gunship.

In the wavering pools of firelight, Vic Gabriel made out the face of his hated enemy. Like some conquering hero, Michael Saunders stood in the fuselage doorway of the gunship as the chopper hovered over the street for several moments, scanning the flaming ruins with his predatory eyes. Searching for his enemies, Saunders—it was obvious to Gabriel—had only found the ruins of war.

From the deep shadows and barely masked in the fireglow, Simms and Dillinger cut loose on the gunship with the one-two punch of the M60 and M16. Sparks whined off the chopper's hull as slugs tattooed metal. A scream and something tumbled from the fuselage, but Gabriel saw that the bloody something wasn't Saunders as it crunched to the street.

More hellfire from the distant black hills descended on the town with no name.

Explosions pealed rolling thunder into the night.

Gabriel lined up his deathsights on the gunship as it moved off, intent on blowing that warbird out of the sky. Some twist of fate prevented him from dealing the decisive blow to Saunders that he wanted. Just as he squeezed off a 40 mm hellbomb from the M203 launcher, an explosion puked through a series of tin shacks nearby. Wreckage hurricaned around Gabriel, banging and slicing off his body and face. As he hit the ground, tasting the spill of blood in his mouth, feeling the deep burning gashes in his face and neck, he heard the explosive impact overhead, glimpsed the saffron flash of fire. He bolted to his feet, moving away from the tracking line of explosions, and saw the warbird spinning, out of control, over the east end of town. The tail section was gone and the fuselage appeared engulfed in fire, the gunship lighting up the sky like some obscene balloon.

But the battle snared Gabriel's attention in another direction then. In the periphery of his sight, Gabriel saw the chopper vanish, then there was a ball of flames geysering into the night from the distance. Was Saunders gone? Was his most hated enemy dead? Slugs stitching the street around Gabriel made the ex–Special Forces warrior focus lethal attention elsewhere.

A line of enemy numbers began surging over the rise in the street, several dozen yards away. With relentless fury, Gabriel, Dillinger, and Simms poured it on with blistering deadly accurate autofire. Gabriel and Dillinger threw 40mm grenades into the charging enemy. Explosions hurtled ragdoll figures into the crackling walls of fire. M60 machine-gun fire dropped men dead where they stood. But they kept coming, wave after wave of gunmen boiling up over the rise, surging past their fallen comrades. It would be suicide to make a stand against that many guns, Gabriel knew. They killed ten, twelve, and two dozen more popped up almost right away to replace the dead.

"Move it out!" Gabriel yelled, and backpedaling, triggering his M16, and expending clip after clip but dropping the enemy in steady droves, led the fighting withdrawal down the street.

Simms kept hosing down enemy numbers with the steady flaming chatter of his M60. The enemy pealed off, seeking cover, and the three mercs quickly put distance between themselves and their adversaries. Return fire from a distance followed the three mercs down the street like an angry swarm of carnivorous insects.

The mortar barrage had ceased. Firelight bathed the twisted bodies up the street, and smoke drifted over the buildings in thick black curtains. Muzzles spat pencil-tip flames through the darkness and slugs tore into the earth

*around the mercs. They fired on the run, but kept the
enemy pinned down.*

Simms and Dillinger cut across the street, caught up
with Gabriel.

"What now?" Dillinger yelled over the stuttering
autofire in the distance.

Gabriel led them toward the jungle. Beyond a low-
lying adobe hut, he spotted the figure. Thanks to the
flickering firelight that consumed a nearby building, he
made out the figure of Inessa. She stood utterly still, her
hands folded in front of her. There was a strangely serene
expression on her face.

As Gabriel closed down on the woman, she said,
"Follow me. I will lead you from this place of death."

Without question, the babble of angry Spanish striking
their backs, Gabriel, Simms, and Dillinger followed the
woman into the dark bowels of the jungle. Gabriel was
amazed at how swiftly, how confidently Inessa moved for a
blind woman. It was as if she sensed her way along,
unflinching, not hesitating, guided by unseen hands. He
had sight, Gabriel thought, and he couldn't keep pace with
her without swiping away the vines and foliage and wanting
to curse the night.

"Quiet," she said, "and follow me this way."

They did. Moved deep into a cave that was cut into the
high hills. Moved deep into the cave for what became hours
of arduous hiking through darkness, and the stink of
rotting things, and the screech of rats and bats angry at the
intrusion of their home.

It was dawn when they broke free of the cave. The first
light of day washed a dirty gray swath across the sky.
Dirt-grimed, cut and bleeding, but otherwise in one piece,
Gabriel found they had topped a hill overlooking the
jungle. In the distance, he saw the pillars of black smoke
towering into the sky. The town with no name had burned
itself out. But the enemy now swarmed over that town,
looking like ants on honey as they combed through the
wreckage. Gabriel could just make out the shouts and
angry voices of the enemy as they kicked through debris.

And Vic Gabriel spotted him. Saunders. He couldn't

see the face of his enemy at the distance of a couple hundred yards but he could tell it was Saunders. By the way he walked, or, rather, limped. The way he gave orders. The way he moved. In charge. In command. Ready to kill. The tension in his body. The rage in his voice.

"Dammit. Dammit!"

Dillinger moved up beside Gabriel. "What?"

"I thought I had killed the bastard last night," Gabriel rasped.

Inessa stood behind the mercs, her hands folded over her waist. "That one," she said, "the one who is Death, he will not die easy. He will become the greatest single threat to your life in the years ahead, Vic Gabriel."

"Years?" Gabriel snarled. "I wanted him dead yesterday."

"It will not be so easy," she went on. "He will prove to be the greatest single obstacle in your life. He was put here as a test."

"Of what?"

Inessa shrugged. "Only you will be able to determine that, Vic Gabriel. Time and Death have become one and the same thing for the both of you. They will cross paths together and lead you to the remotest most dangerous places on the face of the earth. There will be many battles ahead for you, and for the one who is Death. Your destinies are locked together."

Gabriel didn't know how to take that. He heaved a pent-up breath, exhausted.

"You are one of the very few who is a man of destiny," Inessa said.

"I feel privileged," Gabriel said. "All right," he told Dillinger and Simms, "it's about twenty klicks to the border. Suggest we get our butts in gear and hike it over. Inessa?"

She shook her head. "I stay here. My people will return to the ruins of their homes and they will rebuild the town. It is all they have."

Gabriel nodded. "So be it. Before I leave, I want to thank you again. For putting me back together, and for helping us get out of there last night."

A smile ghosted over her lips. "In the years ahead, if you choose to look back on this day, you may not thank me at all. You may curse what I see ahead for you."

Gabriel turned his attention to the far-reaching jungle to the north. A green rolling wall. Where death possibly awaited the three of them. He started to move off the ridge when Simms called to him.

"Hey, man. What about the rest of my money?"

Anger cut through Gabriel, but when he turned and faced Simms, uncertain how to take the black man, he saw the hard expressions on Simms then Dillenger melt. Then laughter rolled into their eyes. Then Simms and Dillinger laughed, long and hard.

Vic Gabriel couldn't suppress his laughter either. Go ahead, he thought, you bloody bastards, you stand-up balls-out fuckers. Laugh at the devil. Laugh all the way into hell. Laugh it up, because we're alive when by all rights we shouldn't be.

Laugh it up for today.

Because tomorrow might never come.

Laugh on, my friends. We're going to get another chance. Another chance to cry for each other.

Chapter 14

Vic Gabriel was under no illusions about their situation. Unholy, unwanted or even bona fide to-the-bitter-end allies, it was every man for himself. It was lock and load, fire and run.

The four commandos of Eagle Force surged into the thunder and smoke, cutting down anything that moved, with all kinds of allies flanking them and pulling up the rear. Most of the combined strike force under Gabriel's command made it. Some didn't and they died out there on the short stretch of no-man's-land, the earth of the jungle drinking their blood and guts.

Any Sandinista sentry who dared to show himself above the rampart wall was stitched and blasted by autofire that blistered across no-man's-land at a savage and unforgiving rate.

Gabriel and Simms triggered their M203s into the smoking gaping maw where a gate had been but was now filled with soldiers doing their damnedest to crush the invaders with merciless AK47 weapons fire. *El Tigre* and his rebels peppered the wall with grenade and LAWs rocket fire.

Bodies spun away from the jagged edges of the rampart wall under the rocket barrage by Contra rebels. Blood, muck, and bits and pieces of wet meat spattered the ground as Gabriel and his commandos led the charge into the garrison, right on the heels of their 40mm hellbomb twinblasts, smoke and blood and cordite biting into their senses, their ears ringing from the concussive punch of explosions. They ran into a hellzone of utter mayhem as debris rained down around them and men screamed and died all around them.

Pumped up on a wildfire explosion of adrenaline, marching right into the face of death, Gabriel fired on the run, wheeling left and mowing down anything that moved, his M16 chattering and dropping Sandinista soldiers by the threes and fours. Vic Gabriel was far from alone in handing out death sentences. He had plenty of help, but Contras were paying the price, either moving just a fraction of a millisecond too slow or being unlucky enough to have fate punch their tickets. Only the swiftest and most deadly accurate weapons fire denied the Grim One there.

Dutch peeled off to the right, the M60 spitting out flaming streams of man-eating lead, shell casings twirling all around the snarl on the big Afrikaaner's face. Sandinistas screamed and tumbled down the steps leading up to the rampart as the Dutchman turned up the heat and drove dead men into each other like dominoes.

Gabriel put the fat colonel out of his mind, but managed to steal a glimpse of Tilton as he barreled through the boiling caldron of smoke. Despite his enormous size, the Fat Man moved pretty damn good, Gabriel decided. A little speed, a little grace, and the guy sure didn't move like he was hovering somewhere around three hundred and thirty or so pounds. Tilton and his people had the drill down. In, firing, peeling off and stitching the enemy with relentless autofire. Fire, cover, and move. Large numbers of Sandinistas ran down the splintered rampart, leaping over sawtooth shards of planks triggering AK47s on the run.

Dutch moved down beneath the rampart. With his M60 he fired up, punching holes through the wood. Gabriel, Simms, and Dillinger, M203s reloaded, swiftly skirted beneath the rampart.

Out on the courtyard it was total savage war. Contra against Sandinista. Gunship against everyone, zeroing in and bearing down to rip apart anything that moved, anything that stood, ran, or crawled.

Countless flaming muzzles stabbed through the veils of roiling smoke. Explosions raked the courtyard.

The gunships swooped, back and forth, over the

courtyard, miniguns hosing down the Sandinistas, rocket pods unleashing a barrage of death from above that obliterated the machine-gun emplacements. Fuel depots and jeeps and transport trucks were vaporized inside one long tidal wave of fireballs that meshed and sucked up anything and everything in its roiling, shrieking doomsday path.

Gabriel, Simms, and Dillinger paved the way for the strike force on their flank, and *El Tigre* and his rebels took the cue. Firing up with his M16, Gabriel heard the screams as bodies spun and toppled off the rampart. Groins and guts were ripped open by dozens of stammering M16s as lines of 5.56mm slugs marched up and down the rampart, chewing up wood and flesh with voracious lead locust swarms.

The going was anything but easy for Gabriel and his people.

Unyielding return fire was directed at the invaders. Slugs sparked and whined off the stone clumns around Eagle Force. Gabriel moved like a wink of lightning, expended one clip after the other, ducking and dodging the ricochet of sparks beside him. Many of *El Tigre's* men weren't as fortunate. Blasts pealed behind Gabriel. Pivoting, crouching behind a pile of rubble, he saw the explosions hurtle rebels skyward, driving them up and through the ramparts like bowling pins shooting through some flimsy matchbook covering. The Sandinistas weren't short on rocket fireteams, Gabriel realized. Those fireteams slid, dark shadows, through the boiling smoke. Gabriel and his troops directed return rocket fire at those Sandinistas and made them ride the fiery crests of explosions that launched them into the dawn sky downrange.

"Take cover!" Gabriel hollered, realizing they were being targeted by more than just the Sandinistas. The mystery strike force in the gunships had been lining them up in their deathsights, the ex–Special Forces warrior realized.

The gunships scissored, back and forth, over the courtyard, laying down a vicious blanket of aerial fire, front to rear, then flank to flank. The gunships swept back over the walls, then went into hairpin turns and banked in, nose down, for still another strafing run of death and mayhem. The courtyard and large sections of the ramparts were in flame. Countless mutilated sacks were strewn across the ground, draped over rubble. One machine-gun emplacement was hosing down the bulk of *El Tigre*'s force, and Gabriel saw those guys dropping in trios, great chunks of flesh being sheared off their twitching, pirouetting bodies and blood splattering the walls like some bizarre modern painting. Worse, one of the gunships was bearing down on them as the principal target now, parting the mountains of black smoke and tearing into their garrison charge of Gabriel and his troops with combined minigun-and-rocket fire. Gabriel knew the score right then. CIA. They were there and under explicit orders to terminate everyone and anyone. Explosions pounded the earth off to Gabriel's right, and he feared the worst for those Contra rebels. A split second later, he saw the bodies of rebels flung through the smoke and fire as if they were nothing more than broken rag dolls.

Slabs of debris began showering down on Gabriel, banging and slicing off him as he fired out across the courtyard at the surviving .50-caliber machine gunner. Gabriel struck paydirt, and the machine-gun emplacement was silenced by his deadly hand. His grim attention was then diverted to the gunship. Like some giant streaking predatory insect, its miniguns flaming, the gunship came at Gabriel and his troops. He didn't have to give the order to blow that bird out of the sky. They were pinned against the wall as heavy slugs tattooed the stone all up and down the garrison facade.

Almost to a man, whoever was equipped with rocket firepower turned on the chopper with grim deathsights.

Predator became the prey, the hunter the hunted.

M203s chugged in the hands of Gabriel, Dillinger, and Simms. Likewise, Tilton and his mercs unleashed 40mm hellbombs and LAWs rockets spat payloads from the hands of the Contra rebels. As Sandinistas and Contras alike screamed and died and explosions hurled their bodies across the courtyard and wreckage puked and razored through the smoke and flames, the gunship was shredded

in midair by a dozen direct hellbomb strikes, less than fifty
meters from where Gabriel and his commandos held their
ground. A monstrous ball of fire lit the dawn sky with a
blinding glare. Whatever was left of the flaming hulk
slammed into the front wall and vomited broken bloody rag
dolls and jagged metal teeth across no-man's-land.

"*Comandante Gringo!*"

Gabriel wheeled, spotted Poet standing over *El Tigre*.
The Contra leader was down and Gabriel didn't see *El Tigre*
move, not even twitch.

With one gunship down, Iceman knew it was time to
disembark and take this action, man-to-man, hand-to-hand
to whatever force greeted them. There was no doubt they
weren't alone in the invasion. The four mystery mercs had
shown themselves and made an accounting with a fierce
blazing entrance into the garrison. They had helped to cut
the enemy numbers down to almost nothing, but they
weren't going to live to be able to savor victory here,
Iceman determined. Ellis had to come first, Iceman decided, then he would square the tab with the four commandos and he didn't give a damn if the President of the United
States had sent those guys to Nicaragua.

"Set it down!" he roared at the gunship pilot. "Then get
this bird outside the walls, and wait. Give me thirty
minutes! You got that?"

The gunship pilot acknowledged the order.

Iceman's numbers, down to six now, piled in behind
him. The gunship lowered through the smoke. Iceman
peered into the smoke, saw three dark figures running
toward him, and opened up with his M16. He dropped
those men where they stood. As the rotor wash cleared
away some of the smoke around the hot LZ, the Iceman
made out the cellblock in the distance. What he saw there
sent ice down his spine. Someone was doing his damnedest
to tip about a dozen barrels over and send some liquid—
flammable liquid, Iceman feared—down the steps leading
into the cellblock. Iceman had to make sure he took out
Ellis himself, and didn't want any living soul to interfere
with his termination of the principal target.

"Move out!" Iceman bellowed, and led his numbers out onto the courtyard.

Bonano gritted his teeth against the roar in his ears. A series of explosions, almost close enough to kill him, had moments ago knocked him on his ass. Without a doubt, his men had taken the worst of the assault.

But Bonano was going to play it out. His way. Even if it took his last breath, he would win.

He forgot about the ringing in his ears, the pain shooting through his body. One by one, he pushed the drums over, washing wave after wave of gasoline down the stone steps. As he tipped over the last drum, he felt something punch into his lower back. His legs seemed to be chopped out right from under him. He toppled, crying out as fire raced through his body. Blackness wavered in and out of his sight and fought the urge to go under, succumb to death.

But he knew death was coming for him.

He had to deny the enemy. He couldn't die, he thought, allowing them total victory.

El Tigre was dead. Gabriel saw that a dozen or more enemy slugs had chopped up his stomach and chest. He felt the renewed vengeance in the stares of the Contra rebels around him. *El Tigre* had proven himself invaluable in getting them this far. A brave warrior, he had fought to the bitter end, and a spare clip was in his hand. The Contra rebel leader had been in the motion of reloading when he'd been hammered into death.

There was no time to mourn the dead.

Looking out across the courtyard, Gabriel saw the gunship lift off. He counted seven men, vanishing in and out of the wafting clouds of smoke in the distance. They were moving to the cellblock, fast and furious. They were going to kill Ellis and most likely every man in there, Gabriel feared.

Quickly, he led the troops across the slaughterzone. Several Sandinistas on the rampart fired at the surge of invaders, but they were sent crashing into the walls or pitching off the planks to the courtyard by ferocious return fire.

Bloody things that crawled through the smoke were shot once in the head as Gabriel led his strike force toward the cellblock. He looked around for Tilton, then spotted the fat man and his mercs peeling off in another direction. The fat man, Gabriel knew, was in search of his pot of gold at the end of the bloody rainbow. Gabriel put Tilton out of his mind. He would deal with him soon enough. Would have to for Lolita's sake.

"Is there another way in?" Gabriel asked Poet.

"*Sí*."

"Show me."

Gabriel checked the troops. They were down to almost a dozen guns.

Spurred on by his lust to take that million, Tilton ordered his surviving eight guns to hurl everything they had at the Sandinistas guarding the command HQ. Tilton was certain the money was in there, because the enemy put up a bitter last-ditch stand.

"Move in! Move in!" he bellowed, and his men fired on the run, cutting down the Sandinistas where they fought. Tilton felt his lust to secure that money burn deeper as he watched three more of his mercs drop in death. He stayed crouched near the burning hull of a jeep, sweat coursing down his face, crackling flames licking close to him. He would wait until it was safe to advance on his primary, his only objective.

But his mercs quickly, savagely paved the way.

And Tilton followed them to the command HQ, knowing he was too close now to let anything stand in his way. Even his own men were expendable, especially his own men. Hideously wounded Sandinistas kept firing, then they writhed in their own blood and filth as Tilton's mercs swarmed over them, triggering their M16s on full auto and chewing their faces and chests up with a tenacious glee, it seemed. Rosco and Paneras flanked the doorway, then barreled inside.

Tilton ran up on the doorway just as Rosco was kicked

back outside with several blood-gouting holes in his chest and back. Autofire blistered beyond the doorway, then it was eerily silent from inside the command HQ.

Tilton peered around the doorway. Three more bodies and Paneras the Panamaniam lay in twisted attitudes of death. And they were strewn near a wooden chest.

"Cover the door!" Tilton ordered his men.

Quickly, licking his lips, he stood over the trunk. He opened the trunk and stifled a gasp as he stared down at the stacks of hundred-dollar bills, American, before his eyes. He couldn't control the urge to laugh. It was his, all his. He shut the lid and picked up the trunk. He didn't trust any of his mercs to carry that million.

"Let's get outta here."

"How?"

"What the fuck you mean how? I saw that chopper go over the wall. My hunch is that pilot's setting that bird down and waiting for those boys he dropped off. We grab that chopper and get the hell outta here. Move!"

And ex–Army Colonel Hank Tilton followed his surviving mercs through the doorway. For just a second, he considered shooting them, then figured that could wait until they were safely airborne and headed out of Nicaragua.

The Iceman came face-to-face with his principal target. His men had secured the corridor. One flame, though, one little spark would ignite the gasoline he was forced to slosh through. The cellblock would become a hellblock.

The sounds of autofire chattering in the distance outside the cellblock, Iceman looked at Ellis through the iron bars, sized the major up with cold scrutiny. The target was cool, calm. The guy knew. It was over.

Iceman shot the lock off the door with his M16. The door swung out, creaking on rusty hinges.

"Uncle Sam sends his regards, Major," Iceman told Ellis, who just stood at the far corner of the cell, resigned, it seemed, to his fate. "You fucked up."

Iceman knew how he would take care of the other advisers in the cellblock. One flick of his Zippo and the

CIA's ass was covered. He didn't have time, he knew, to march up and down the corridor and fire into the cells and make sure each target was erased.

Ellis stood, stripped to the waist. There was no fear, no anger in his stare. He was beaten, bruised and bleeding still from the punishment.

"So shoot me, you bastard."

Iceman hesitated for a moment. Ellis had only done what his country had asked him to do. It was a shitty thing, Iceman thought, to be asked to have to pay for someone else's sins.

Iceman leveled his M16 on Ellis, squeezed the trigger.

Chapter 15

They came in the back way, firing, M16s set on full-auto slaughter.

Vic Gabriel sent the first target in his sights reeling to the floor, but the guy managed to squeeze off a quick burst with his M16 at whoever was in that cell he had drawn down on. Gabriel feared the worst, dreaded what he would find in that cell.

He had no time to dwell on his worst-case scenario.

Six commandos were pivoting his way and lining him up in their deathsights.

Dillinger, Simms, and Boolewarke bounded down the steps, firing their weapons at the six figures down the corridor. And the surviving Contras of *El Tigre*'s force joined in the brutal burial of the mystery commandos in one long stammering fusillade of autofire as they poured into the cellblock to a man.

It was no mystery to Gabriel who and what they had just sent on their way. A hit team, sent to Nicaragua by the CIA to cover their snafu. Everything had just become ancient brutal history. The arms deal. Attila's garrison. And Vic Gabriel feared the worst for Lolita but hoped for the best. As long as he was alive, he would do everything in his power, move heaven, earth, and hell to get back to her. And if she was . . . he didn't want to think about it. Too many had suffered too much for too little already.

Quickly, the stench of gasoline biting into his senses, he closed on the first cell. Dead limbs twitched up and down the corridor. The mystery strike force had ceased to exist, but Gabriel discovered they had scored victory.

Vic Gabriel found Major Ben Ellis lying in a pool of his own blood. Pain, grief, and rage tore through him as he crouched over the man who had saved his life, so many lifetimes ago, in Southeast Asia. Gabriel suddenly found himself locked up in his own private world of anguish and fury.

Ellis looked up at Gabriel through glazed eyes. "Y-you . . . Gabriel . . ."

The guy almost smiled. Almost, but he groaned and spat up blood. Ellis was gut-shot and dying fast.

"Smell . . . it . . . gasoline . . ."

"Easy, Major. I'm taking you home."

"Forget . . . it . . . I'm dying . . . won't make it . . . the gas . . . they're gonna . . . light the whole . . . frigging . . . place up . . . just . . . don't let me . . . burn alive . . . you squared it . . . then. . . ."

He knew he was on his last breath. He was covered in blood, but he was momentarily surprised that there was no pain. He had been shot in the lower back and his guts were leaking out through his splayed fingers.

Miguel Horchiba Bonano was a dead man, and he knew it. He heard the distant crackles of fire, knew the garrison was destroyed, would be amazed if any of his men were still alive and fighting. He heard nothing but the roaring in his ears, concentrated on nothing but his desire to set the gasoline on fire.

He fumbled in his pants pockets, pulled out a Zippo. He snapped the cover back and flicked the wheel. A flame danced to life. He had heard the autofire down in the cellblock, knew he could take out a good number of the enemy responsible for his death.

Responsible for terminating his command of the zone. All was lost. Almost all was lost. Even in death he would have mounted at least a half victory.

Bonano tossed the Zippo into the pool of gas. He sighed his last breath on earth, and blackness took him as the fire whooshed to life. Bonano died with a twisted half smile on his lips.

* * *

The cellblock became an instant hellblock.

Gabriel hauled Ellis out of the cell, the major draped over his shoulders in a fireman's carry, as the fire raced at him.

The fear of being burned alive burst fresh adrenaline through Gabriel. As the flames washed down the corridor, a series of explosions shook the ground beneath his feet. He took the first two steps, the Contras surging out of the cellblock, hammering each other through the doorway, as fire breathed for Eagle Force. Simms and Dillinger grabbed Ellis off Gabriel's shoulders. Together, they spilled through the doorway, tumbled to the ground as the fire blazed, then stopped halfway up the steps.

Then Gabriel smelled the stench of roasting flesh, heard the bone-chilling screams of men being burned alive. Those screams tore through his head.

"B-bastard . . ."

He looked down at Ellis. For what seemed like an eternity, the shrill wailing hammered at his back, then, one by one, the screams ceased.

"He . . . didn't . . . have to do . . . that . . . bastard. . . ."

But the Sandinista comandante had. And if he was still alive, Gabriel would make him pay the price.

Simms, Dillinger, and Boolewarke looked back down the steps. To a man, rage burned in their eyes over the senseless barbarism of torching those held captive under the Sandinista comandante. Smoke poured out of the cellblock, breathing a nauseating stench into the air.

"Hey . . . soldier . . ."

Gabriel looked deep into Ellis's eyes.

"Dutch!"

Boolewarke moved beside Gabriel.

"Can you do something for him?"

Then Gabriel heard the rasping sigh. He didn't have to look down to know that Ellis was dead, but he did. A blank stare sought him out. Gently, he closed Ellis's eyelids.

Gabriel squeezed his own eyes shut, pinching the bridge of his nose with his thumb and forefinger. The mission was a wash. He sensed his commandos and the Contra rebels standing around him, but he was lost in his own private world of anguish. He'd kept Ellis from burning alive, but the major was still dead, and that was the bottom line. If you called that squaring a tab . . . *Dammit!* He let the pain tear through him, felt it ripping to the core of his soul for long moments.

Suck it up, soldier, keep going, dig, dig deep and pull it out. There's still a life hanging in the balance, a life still counting on you to pull through. No time to dwell on this insanity. No time at all. Time is up.

When he looked at his commandos there was new fire burning in his eyes.

"The Fat Man," Gabriel growled. "I want him."

Major Ivan Kubchkin knew he was looking at total disaster. Huge billowing clouds of smoke blossomed over the shattered front wall of the garrison and blackened the sky, shutting out the faintest traces of early-morning light. The pitched battle was in its death throes, he was certain. The enemy had scored a major victory in the zone. Only moments ago, all autofire had ceased from inside those walls. Some terrible shrill screams had pierced the walls of smoke blanketing the jagged holes in the garrison facade, but they had lingered in the air for only a few moments. Now there was only a hollow silence ringing the garrison. Kubchkin sniffed at the air, recognized the stench of burning flesh. He wasn't sure what he and his commandos and the handful of Sandinista soldiers under his command were faced with.

He would find out.

The gunship had landed moments ago on the stretch of no-man's-land.

From the edge of the jungle tree line, he led the dash to the lone gunship. He forged into the rotor wash, prepared to kill anybody inside the chopper.

The gunship's pilot and co-pilot stepped out of the cockpit just as Kubchkin reached the fuselage doorway. With his AK47, he shot them dead where they stood.

As he turned, he saw his commandos and the Sandin-

istas gathering near the warbird. He was about to curse
their lack of common tactical combat sense for bunching up
when the first of several explosions tore through their
numbers and kicked them as broken bloody stick figures
back into the jungle.

"Tilton!"

Gabriel was the first one through the boiling smoke of
the front gate. His M16 was locked and loaded and he was
drawing down on the Fat Man. The ex–Special Forces
warrior took the battlefront in at an eyeblink. A new strike
force had converged on the chopper and Tilton and his
mercs had come up on them from behind, decimated their
numbers with a quick flash of autofire and grenade bombardment. Fresh corpses littered no-man's-land. More
bodies, Gabriel determined, were also going to stack up on
the conveyor belt of death.

Weapons poised to fire, Simms, Dillinger, and Boolewarke were right on Gabriel's heels.

Panic flashed through Tilton's eyes. He carried the
trunk on his shoulders and Gabriel knew without asking, by
judging the fear in Tilton's voice, that the Fat Man had
found his million.

"No . . . don't shoot, you fool!" Tilton cried out.
"We're rich men! We're rich! We can cut a deal! I'll split it
with you, for Christ sake! Just don't shoot. . . ."

Tilton's men swung their M16s toward Eagle Force.
They were only a few steps away from the safety of the
gunship fuselage. They would never make those few steps.

"*Nooooo!*" Tilton roared in a blind fury and terror as
the dark dawn of realization sank in. "*Don't!*"

And Eagle Force opened up on Tilton and his cutthroats. Dutch's M60 blazed, and the M16s of Gabriel,
Simms, and Dillinger ripped free with a long stammering
death knell. Tilton's surviving mercs went down under the
lead onslaught, and the Fat Man was opened up from navel
to chest, hurled into the gunship fuselage. The trunk
slammed to the ground, burst open. Instantly, bills were
sucked up by the rotor wash and hurled, a green cyclone of
countless American dollars, around the gunship.

Combat senses still on full alert, Gabriel led his commandos to the gunship. The only thing he found was death and more death. A hurricane of American dollars ripped around him and his commandos. Turning, Gabriel saw the surviving Contra rebels warily trudging through the smoke. They were down to ten men. Only Poet and Zorro, *El Tigre's* most trusted fighters, had survived the raging battle within the walls of Attila's hellhole. Don Juan, John Wayne, and Rat Man had all perished with their brothers-in-arms.

"You find him?" Gabriel asked Poet.

"*Sí*, Comandante Gringo. It was Attila. He is dead. We tossed his stinking carcass into the fire. It was him who started the blaze that burned those men alive."

Gabriel had no time to reflect on the moment. It was time only to find out if another dreaded truth were to have a dark light shed upon it. Lolita.

Gabriel and his commandos ignored the whirling storm of American dollars. For the briefest of moments, Poet and his rebels eyed the money.

Then Gabriel felt the earth tremble beneath him. He looked at his commandos, at Poet. The vibrations grew stronger and he heard a rumble roll over the jungle.

"What the hell?" Dillinger rasped.

"The Sleeping Lion," Poet said, and Gabriel heard the note of fear in the rebel's voice.

"The what?" Gabriel said.

"It is a volcano," Poet answered. "Near San Pedro. The Sleeping Lion . . . he is awake. They say it will explode any day. Perhaps today . . . but I pray I am long gone from this world before the Sleeping Lion, he explodes."

Poet scanned the sky, and Gabriel could tell the rebels were terrified of the Sleeping Lion.

"He's not the only one set to explode," Vic Gabriel growled, and ordered everyone into the gunship.

Chapter 16

Vic Gabriel was the first one to disembark from the gunship as it touched down in a small clearing. Bright sunlight burned down on the jungle. Gabriel checked his Rolex. Still more than three hours until high noon, but he feared time had already run out on Lolita. He felt the earth tremble beneath his feet, heard the distant rumble. The Sleeping Lion, he knew, was waking up. Not even the forces of nature, though, would stop him from stalking and killing any man who harmed Lolita in way, shape, or form. If she was dead and if that volcano erupted and buried half of Nicaragua under a sea of molten lava, he would just as soon die there in the jungle. It had been awhile since he had been pushed to the edge of insanity like this. To the point where if it all went down in despair, and he no longer cared . . . it would be a long way back.

Gabriel was swiftly forging ahead into the jungle, M16 in hand, a half klick away from the truth in San Pedro, when he heard Dillinger call out.

"Vic!"

Gabriel stopped, turned, and looked at Dillinger. Simms and Boolewarke gathered around Gabriel and the ex-P.I. Sweat coursed down the faces of the commandos, washing away some of the dried blood and dirt that caked their expressions. Gabriel was vaguely aware that Dillinger and Simms had taken slugs along their ribs during the savage fighting inside Attila's hell. They moved slowly, gingerly, and he knew they were in pain. He was in pain, too, but of a different and perhaps worse kind.

"Vic," Dillinger implored, "you go charging in there, they might just panic and kill her."

"There's no way to finesse this," Gabriel growled. "Give me the lead, but cover my ass. I'll call it as it goes down."

That was it. That was all he said. All he needed to say. It was going to go down his way or no way at all. Life or death, no in-between. His commandos knew better than to try and talk him into any other course of action.

As Gabriel pulled away, his commandos just looked at each other, resigned, it seemed, to let their leader do it his way.

And Gabriel led the way through the jungle, his commandos and the surviving Contra rebels right on his heels. His heart pounding with fear, his mind steeled with grim resolve, Gabriel tried to force himself to sweep aside all emotions. It was no good. He realized he wanted to save the woman, his woman, if he could, more than anything he had wanted in a long, long time. It seemed every time he went in to save somebody he lost them. So many names stacked up on the headstone of his war—friends, family . . .

That was his track record. He didn't know why it always went down that way, but it did, and it hurt, a hurt that maybe he had been denying himself from feeling for too long. He didn't think he could stomach losing Lolita. She had lost too much already, and she didn't deserve to lose her life now. Not after what she had been through, what he had unwittingly put her through to endure in her silent, strong, stoic way. She had seen his pain, had listened to his reasoning with a strong and open heart, and had forgiven him for abandoning her so long ago. An abandonment he had committed through no real fault of his own. Fate had simply jerked and blown him around, like so much loose paper sucked up in a strong wind. It was time to resolve the past, he thought, then wondered if he was being spurred on by so much guilt. He decided he wasn't. Lolita deserved better than suffering through the rest of her life in the squalor of San Pedro. They deserved each other.

They had survived their pasts and so had earned their future.

The earth trembled, and the sky rumbled in a violent peal that shook the jungle. The Sleeping Lion then slept.

An eerie silence greeted Gabriel and his troops as they walked into San Pedro. The bright blue sky was dark with the ominous shapes of countless buzzards. Vic Gabriel felt his heart become a cold, dead thing in his chest as he took in the slaughter.

"*Madre de Dios*," Poet said in a harsh whisper. The surviving Contra rebels just stared at the massacre with expressions numbed and frozen into disbelief.

The slaughter stretched throughout San Pedro. A slaughter so complete, so terrible, there could be no forgiveness anywhere at any time for the men who had committed this atrocity. Bodies of men, women, and children littered the streets, and the buzzards gorged themselves on the dead meat of man and animal alike. Flies teemed and crawled over the unfeeling flesh of the dead, swarms so huge and so alive they looked like thick black blankets that rippled.

Gabriel's mind raced with fear. Where to start looking, if they were even there? Where?

A shrill scream suddenly knifed the air.

Gabriel whirled toward the church.

"You bitch! You goddamn bitch, I'll kill you! I'll kill you!"

Gabriel felt rooted to the ground, then, recognizing Lolita's voice, he bolted toward the church. The shrill male screams and cursing and threats boomed over the heaps of rubble, ripped over the dead bodies Gabriel ran past—like cannon fire blasting right at him. Fear turned to terror.

Autofire rang out.

Noooooooo! Gabriel heard his mind scream, leaping over the rubble, kicking through the splintered ruins of the church door.

What he found burned nausea into his throat, and he felt his heart sink totally, completely into the bottom of his stomach. The world spun in his eyes and he thought he would topple, but rage kept him standing. Rage and cold vengeance. He heard the bootsteps of his own men pounding over the earth behind him, but all of his grim and fury-filled attention was riveted on the altar.

There, he felt his heart begin to cave and want to succumb with despair to the final, sickening twist of fate. Somehow, he forced iron into his will, knowing there was only one thing left to do, only one thing left that he could do. There was a bloody thing on the altar with long black hair, and he saw it through a burning mist. So overcome with murderous rage, Gabriel couldn't even focus reality on that thing being Lolita.

But it was.

Two monsters wheeled in his direction. Tears streamed down from a monster face, and that thing had its hands clasped over a bloody crotch. A weapon muzzle began to stab through the fiery veil of mist in Gabriel's eyes. He clenched his teeth so hard he thought he would break every single tooth off in his mouth. There was a roaring in his ears and then he did the only thing left he could do.

Vic Gabriel let the M16 in his hands rip. He emptied the entire thirty-round clip into those two monsters, chopped them up into gut-spewing, blood-gouting meat. For the buzzards. For the worms.

For the goddamn devil in hell.

The last round spent, he felt himself just stand there on wooden legs. A statue. Empty. Unfeeling. Unaware of the noise behind him, the lingering echo of the killing shots in his head.

The three commandos raced into the church and pulled up behind their leader.

A sound of despair rasped out of Zac Dillinger's mouth, and he hung his head.

For two days it had been just about the only news story on television and it had captured the headlines around the world. The Sleeping Lion had finally erupted, as experts had recently predicted it would, and buried more than a quarter of Nicaragua and parts of Costa Rica, Honduras, and El Salvador under a sea of molten lava. Ash and lava had been spewed from the volcano and been hurled as far south as Colombia and Peru and Bolivia. The streaming curtains of fine volcanic dust had blotted out rays of the sun, lowering temperatures by as much as ten degrees throughout the entire Western Hemisphere. Managua had been buried under a fiery rain of death and not a square foot of the capital of Nicaragua had escaped the wrath of the Sleeping Lion. Emergency relief from all over the free world was pouring into Nicaragua. It was all too little, too late. It was estimated that as many as a half-million people may have been killed by the Sleeping Lion.

Vic Gabriel had been killed in Nicaragua, but in another way. With his commandos he had returned to Fortress Eagle Isle in the Caribbean. Back there, he couldn't bring himself to help in burying the dead of San Pedro, not even Lolita, especially Lolita. The entire ordeal had left him numb, a vacant thing whose soul had been sucked out by the horror he had left behind.

He had managed to stem back the tears, shut off the pain during the flight to Jamaica then the boat ride out to their private island. That was until he had returned to the island. It had all seemed to hit home, burn deep into his soul as soon as he was alone. Then, in the darkness, he had gone off by himself and wept. And wept for what seemed like an eternity. Wept so hard, so long, and so bitterly that when he had pressed his fingers to his closed eyes, he had wanted to gouge those eyes out so he wouldn't have to see the world anymore. Overwhelmed by it all, he just let the pain consume him, hoping his grief would finally cleanse him of his pain. It hadn't. Then he had tried to crush his agony with liquor. He drank and drank. And drank. And wept some more, locked up in his own private hell, not wanting to see or know any of it. Hoping they would drop the bomb, hoping the world would perish before he opened his eyes again. To survive and to endure, he told himself. That was all that was left.

He had come so close to having so much. Only to have lost it. What could he have done differently? What, goddammit, what?

For two days, Vic Gabriel stayed away from any human

contact. He even began to despise himself. He had been nicked and scratched and cut by shrapnel and flying lead at the garrison of Attila. He endured his physical pain, even enjoyed it. The body heals, but if and when the soul dies inside, there is no coming back, there is no return to living.

Vic Gabriel believed, or told himself, that he would be back. He would restore his soul and return to the living, scarred and damaged, but stronger and better for the hell he had burned in.

Now, as the sun set, he sat in the sand and looked out across the Caribbean, staring at the dark shadows stretching over the turquoise waters of the reef. He only came down to the water when it was dark, or when night was approaching. He had found himself loathing the light of day, and in some strange way, he found himself even loathing his own men. Loathing his own life.

These feelings would pass, he told himself, and took another healthy pull off the bottle. Two empty bottles of rum lay beside him, and he found himself loathing his desire to drown his pain in an alcohol-induced stupor. What else was he going to do? The surf crashed gently against the beach, and the warm waters washed up under his feet. He felt nothing right then, except a deep and all-consuming bewilderment. Repeatedly he had asked himself, *Why? And how?*

Why, indeed. It made no sense. None of it. The mission to bail Major Ellis out of Nicaragua and help the United States save face could be seen as a complete and dismal failure, he thought. If there had been any good in it, he failed to see it. Right then, he didn't want to see it. Maybe in time . . .

"Vic?"

Gradually, he became aware of Dillinger's voice. He looked up, and Dillinger squatted beside him. He had beaten himself up enough, Gabriel thought. Time to get it up and get on with it. If he stayed where he was, then they would have ultimately won. Whoever the hell they were anyway.

Gabriel offered Dillinger the bottle, and his friend took

it and chugged a good swallow. "You three have left me alone long enough. Time to come back."

Dillinger seemed to be choosing his words carefully, and Gabriel could sense his friend's unease.

The ex–Special Forces warrior stared out to sea. "She had our son. He died and I never even got the chance to know him . . . not for a second. Never even laid eyes on him. She didn't even have a picture of him, it was like he never even existed. And because of me, he didn't. I just left her there, so long ago. By herself, with our son. Waiting, hoping I would come back. Left her, to go chase another horror that seemed so damn important at the time. I didn't tell any of you. I couldn't."

Pain welled up in Dillinger's eyes. He didn't know what to say. "I could tell . . . she meant a lot to you. She must have been some lady, old man. I'm sorry it turned out the way it did. All of us are. No matter what happened or is going to happen, you're our man, Vic. Always."

Gabriel snorted softly, shook his head. "Why is it almost nothing works out the way you want it to you, the way you know it can. Is it because we don't try hard enough? Is it because we really don't want what we know we should have? Is it because we all know inside that all of this is going to pass soon enough and the effort we expend to get somewhere, to get what we want, is not really worth it? That it's all going to be gone anyway? And what's left? What's here is what's left. But what is it all anyway? What? What?"

"I don't know. I don't know," Zac Dillinger quietly said, and joined his friend in staring out to sea, gazing off into the infinite expanse of an unforgiving world.

And Vic Gabriel heard his own words echo through the tortured abyss of his soul.

What is it all anyway?

FASTEN YOUR SEATBELTS . . .

EAGLE FORCE IS BACK—
IN THEIR MOST EXCITING ADVENTURE
YET!

EAGLE FORCE #8: SUPER EDITION

HELL'S MARCH
by
Dan Schmidt

Turn the page for an exciting preview of HELL'S
MARCH, the EAGLE FORCE SUPER EDI-
TION.

EAGLE FORCE: *They're coming at you*!
Look for Eagle Force wherever Bantam Books
are sold.

It could all come crashing and burning down around them, but they had come too far now to turn back. The team was committed, and they were set to take down their biggest load yet, a haul that would set them up for life in bigshot, high-flying, grand-living style.

Seeing something like this through, from its planning genesis to its brutal execution, had never been a problem for DEA Agent Bud Carlson. They had done it twice before, but now they were set to taste their biggest score, and the mere thought of the cash benefits at the end of the line caused Carlson more than a little anxiety. He realized he was sweating as he caught a whiff of himself on the warm breeze that breathed in off the Miami River and stirred through the car. If caught, they were finished, but a winner never considers the possibility of failure, does he, and so Carlson crushed any feelings of worry and self-doubt he had with a steely mind-set and resolve to get the job done. Bang, bang, in and out. That was how it was going to go down. Silk and cream. Thunder and lightning. Carlson thought he was getting high off the adrenaline rush alone, then felt the icy shiver of fear go down his spine as he sat in the unmarked Plymouth, gazing across the deserted boat yard, fingering his salt-and-pepper mustache. A few lights bathed a fraction of the yard and the surrounding wharves, but the area around the target was locked in by a Stygian gloom.

The night watchman had already been taken care of, paid off with a fat wad of Ben Franklins to make himself scarce, see no evil, hear no evil. In the distance, across the short stretch of no-man's-land, Carlson scoured the dark hulls of the rusty Panamanian and South American freighters, checked the smaller bulks of yachts and Bahamian coasters through a slit-eyed gaze. They were berthed, silent, sulking behemoths in the blackness of night, unmanned, unattended—all except the Panamanian shrimper. Nothing moved out of the yard beyond the chain-link fence. For a moment, Carlson listened to the soft hum of bilge pumps and generators, trying to soothe his nerves, then felt the tension come roaring back, filling his ears with a noise like cannon fire. He spotted the two shadows on the deck of the shrimper, sliding off into the murky recesses of the steel hull. They were there, all right, setting things in motion, getting ready to off-load their cargo of poison. The twinkling Miami skyline was like some ghostly pale aurora far beyond the boat yard, a looming shimmering distant backdrop, overwhelming and overseeing one of countless smugglers' drop points and coves that hemorrhaged Florida with more than a billion dollars' worth of cocaine a week. From Colombia to transshipment points in the Bahamas and Panama and down the Miami River, this was smugglers' lane, Carlson knew, having worked south Florida for nine long, hard unrewarding years as a DEA special agent. Tonight it was the end of the line for a handful of those smugglers. Small fish, death-merchant delivery men in a monster ring of modern-day alchemists who would be missed only because they could provide a clue about the mystery that was about to unfold here, were soon to become food for the bigger fish.

"I tell ya, the old men by the sea aren't going like this. I got this bad feeling, Bud, that they're going to finger us, and if that happens our days in Miami are numbered in single digits. Okay, so we've managed it twice, but bad things come in threes." Grunting, he added, "That's what my horoscope said today. Be careful of things that come in threes. So I'm worried, so what? Aren't you?"

"Worried about you worrying. You worry too much, pal, that's your problem. And stop talking about things in such romantic horseshit terms. Those old men got the biggest illegal action going the world's ever seen. I don't feel sorry for them, not one iota, and I don't worry about what 'the old men by the sea' are or aren't going to do. When you start romanticizing, your nerves show, and when your nerves show, you start sweating."

"Can't help it. We're playing a bad game with some

bad people. Christ, and we're supposed to be the good guys, the front-line troops in this war against the narcoterrorists."

"There you go again, romanticizing, putting everything in glittery fairy-tale terms. Good guy versus bad guy. Forget that crap. You've been poisoned by your own romanticism. Look at it like it's just another job, another sting."

"Can't help it."

"Jesus."

Carlson had a big-boned face, broad nose, and high forehead, and when he scowled at his partner, Jake Polanski, his features looked as if they had been carved from granite. Carlson was a big, broad-shouldered man, topping two hundred pounds and not an ounce of it fat; he could have been a linebacker in the NFL. In fact, that had been his dream, long ago, when he had been in college, but bad knees and a bad attitude, an unwillingness to be a team player, had shattered that dream and sent the pro scouts looking elsewhere for somebody else who had that intangible something, something more than just sheer ability on the gridiron. Somehow Bud Carlson had managed to make a dream of a different kind work for him in the DEA.

"Man, I sometimes wonder if you got any idea who we've been taking these loads from. Or maybe you don't care."

"Fuck them," Carlson rasped at his partner. Feeling the anger rising from the depths of his guts, he glanced at his partner. Polanski was a slightly built man, with sharp features like a ferret, and somehow those features, Carlson decided, fit his partner's almost constant nervous disposition. Carlson knew exactly who and, more importantly, what Polanski referred to by "the old men." Polanski was acting like a nervous old woman, Carlson thought, and fought to stifle the urge to snap out at his partner with a tongue-lashing that would make the devil himself cringe.

"The Cartel can shift their operation wherever they want to, pal," Carlson said, and riveted his attention back to the targeted Panamanian shrimper. "Venezuela, Ecuador, Brazil, or any friggin' banana republic in Central America, don't make a damn bit of difference. The old men may be hunkered down in Cartagena or Barranquilla or Santa Marta or Caracas, soaking up some sunshine by the shore, thinking they're safe from the reach of that big Andean strategy right now, but they're still on the run and they're scared of losing what they've got, and if they want to stay in business, they're gonna play ball with us—if it even comes down to them figuring this out. We just got lucky enough to grab a few of their errand boys by the nuts and get the intel we needed to make us a few scores. Gallega is filling the belly of some big fish out at sea by now, and thanks to him we're here, looking at a huge white pot of gold. How's he going to tell the old men anything now, huh? Besides, dead Colombian runners aside, I've covered our tracks with enough smoke screens the Cartel will be a memory a hundred years from now before anybody figures it out. Hell, and even if they do catch on, you think they're gonna send somebody up here to complain to the DEA that somebody's stealing their coke? A hit team, that what you're worried about? Shit. I'll deal with that, too. Fuck 'em, fuck 'em all. They got so much shit flooding into south Florida, you think they're really going to miss a few scores? We can seize six or seven tons of the shit and they can just shrug it off as a small cost of doing business."

Polanski snorted, shaking his head. "A few scores, you say. We got a ton, maybe more, of ninety-percent marching dust on that shrimper staring down at us, if Gallega was correct. Enough flake that somebody's going to miss it. How I got talked into this . . . I'll never know."

"How? I'll tell ya how, partner. You got your sickness, too, just like the rest of us. You should've thought about all this before you got into your bookie for fifty large."

A pained look crept into Polanski's eyes. "This is it for me, Bud. My last one. I got a wife and kids, I can't take this action anymore. My nervous system is shot."

"I already told ya, this *is* it. No more after tonight. We just make sure our asses are covered and you know what we gotta do to cover 'em. Let me handle it. You just find that shit on board and do it quick."

"We've still got that other problem."

Carlson heaved a sigh. "It's being looked into, you know that, dammit. When we stash this load and get back to Miami, I'll make some phone calls and get us an update, if that'll calm your nerves. I'm tellin' ya, you start sweating, somebody's going to notice. So stop the worrying, all right?"

"Yeah, yeah."

Just then the walkie-talkie on the seat between the two agents crackled.

"Sea Wolf to Sea Breeze. Come in."

Carlson picked up the walkie-talkie. "Yeah. Talk."

"We're in position."

"All right, this is it. D-Day. Go!"

Carlson's hand streaked inside his jacket and pulled out a 9mm Beretta, and a moment later he had a silencer screwed onto the weapon. "Hit the lights and make sure you got a silencer on your piece."

As Carlson jumped out of the car, he saw the headlights of their Plymouth blink once. Down the deserted street, two vans, their lights off, gunned their engines and shot toward the chain-link fence. Carlson was through the gate, the vans roaring up behind him, when he saw his team of six men hit the gangway running. Silenced M16s and Berettas fanned the gloom, and shadows converged on more shadows at the top of the gangway. It went down so quick, the shrimper's crew just stood at the top of the gangway and on the deck, frozen in panic and terror.

"Freeze! DEA! Get your hands up!" Carlson bellowed, topping the gangway. "Move it, inside and get the shit!" he ordered his people. Waving his Beretta at the frightened faces of the six crewmen in front of him, Carlson ordered them down the gangway. "Keep moving. Toward the wharf. Don't say a word."

Carlson heard the shouting and commotion from inside the shrimper, a muffled·roar of voices, but no gunfire. Good. It was going down smoothly. Silk and cream. Thunder and lightning. Now for the dirty part.

When he lined the crew up on the wharf, Carlson began shooting each man in the face, once. Two tried to bolt, fleeing down the wharf, small shadows bounding off into the darkness. Carlson drew down on them with a two-handed grip, squeezed off four slugs, and sent lethal rounds sneezing off into the night. Downrange, he struck flesh, and two figures toppled off into the Miami River.

"We got it."

Wheeling, Carlson saw Polanski hustling the captain of the shrimper toward him at gunpoint.

"You can't do this! You just murdered my crew! Who are you? You aren't DEA."

Carlson grinned. "Captain Ramero, welcome to Miami. Gallega sends his best . . . from the bottom of the Atlantic."

And Carlson shot Captain Ramero in the face. As Ramero crumpled to the wharf, his dead weight slamming wood and sending violent vibrations beneath his feet, Carlson rolled the dead captain off the wharf with his foot and dropped him into the black waters of the river. Corpses bobbed to the surface, then began floating away from the wharf. One more problem to take care of in the yard, Carlson thought.

Carlson leveled an anxious gaze on Polanski. "How much?"

"It was between the two rear bulkheads," Polanski answered. "They were just starting to pull it out. At first glance, I'd say as much, maybe more than we expected. One hell of a lot of powder."

"All right," Carlson said, looking toward the two vans parked at the bottom of the gangway. "Get that shit loaded up. Renaldo!" he barked at another man with a DEA jacket. "Find that watchman. One bullet. Make it clean and quick and quiet. We're outta here."

Polanski lowered his head, his Beretta hanging by his side in a limp grasp. "Jesus."

Carlson didn't have time to calm jittery nerves. He brushed past his partner and growled, "What did I tell ya about sweating?"

Two kilos of Colombian snow and fifty thousand large in cold hard cash. That was how it had all started eight months ago. One CI, a confidential informant, had led Carlson and his team onto the trail of a middleweight

Cubano dealer in the mean streets of Little Havana. Where crack and coke were sold on every street corner in open defiance of a law that had long since proven itself impotent in the face of a national epidemic. Where a whole lot of the so-called good guys had long since decided, *If you can't beat them . . .*

Standing behind the glass-fronted mahogany bar in the team's high-rise beachfront condo in Miami, their safe-house, Bud Carlson poured himself a stiff bourbon and water on the rock. Ice rocks. Another kind of rock was being passed around in waterpipes.

Sipping his drink and firing up a foot-long Cuban stogie with his Zippo, Carlson checked the scene with an eye of mild disapproval. They'd come a long way, he decided, since those early days when CIs led them onto the scent of midlevel dealers and then those CIs and dealers turned up in backstreet garbage bins with one bullet through their brains. It had been so easy. Log half of the cash and coke into evidence, stash the rest. And who was going to believe a dope pusher's word against the word of Uncle Sam's finest law in the land? And even if dead pushers are found at the scene of a bust, *Hell, Cap'n, they had guns. Just look around at this place. We walked into a friggin' armory here and they just panicked and went for the nearest piece. We had no choice. They left us no choice.*

So log it that way. But more like lock and load, take the white gold, and run and stash the cash.

Carlson looked around the living room, puffing contentedly on his smoke. Marble floors and plush white wall-to-wall carpet. Palm trees and big mirrors with fancy gold trim. It was all flash and glitter, just like the bullshit life-styles of the scum they tracked down and ripped off, he thought, but there was one big glaring difference. They had the law on their side. They were protected. They were covered. In both small and big places, from top to bottom. It was the perfect scam, a con man's dream. They had the life.

Now it was party time. Worry about tomorrow when tomorrow comes.

At least a half-dozen women, all nubile young beach

bunnies in various states of disrobe and dishevelment, lounged or roamed the condo. They were hitting the pipes with small propane torches and Carlson noticed a couple of them were starting to get that glazed zombie look that told him they were right at the edge of psychotic paranoia. He only tolerated this kind of bullshit because he was the man with the candy and they would come to him later, begging for another rock. That was when he would collect on their tab and have them hitting another kind of pipe. By then, they would do anything. *Anything*. Carlson had always hated the sound of freebasing, that loud crackling sound when fire hits the coke rock and melts it down into smoke. It sounded like death. At the moment, that was all he was hearing—death. Then he heard the massive snuffling down at the end of the bar. Turning, drink and stogie in hand, he saw one of his men, Tom Overton, whiffing up a few fat lines from the glass bartop, the kind of lines that would have killed a dinosaur, Carlson thought. Overton went, "Aaaaah," wiped his nose, and stood there, grinning like an idiot, down at his reflection. Almost right away, Overton got that look in his eyes, locked into a state of euphoria blasting him all the way to Jupiter and points beyond in the solar system on a snow rocket ride into oblivion. To this day, Carlson knew that science still couldn't figure out exactly why the cocaine molecule acts on the pleasure centers of the brain the way it does. Carlson had no intention of trying to unravel the mystery himself.

"What a life, huh, Bud babe, what a life." Overton sighed, the idiot grin frozen on his lips. "Easy street from here on out. We got it made. We figured we were looking at a ton and a half easy. Step on it two or three times and God only knows how many hundreds of millions we'll be fattening up our accounts down in the Bahamas with."

"I wish you'd back off that shit altogether, Tommy," Carlson rasped. "You know how I feel about that. Shit's poison, but you treat it like it's gold. You start looking around on the floor for crumbs later, I'll kick your ass. Read me?"

Overton hit another line. "What's your problem? This stuff *is* gold—hell, it's worth three, four times more than gold by the ounce, depending on how much shake it's jacked around with. You talk like all of a sudden we're doing something wrong. This is your show, remember, you organized it, called all the right moves. You sure don't mind taking the money for it."

Carlson didn't need that kind of criticism from his people. He felt his hand tremble with rage as he stuck the stogie in his mouth. For a moment, he fixed his gaze on a scantily clad blonde standing over by the double sliding doors and let his fury recede before he did something he would later regret as he let his eyes wander over her body from head to toe. She was just staring out to sea with a lost look on her face, like she was wishing she was somewhere else, maybe all the way across the Atlantic, removed from this insanity, maybe wondering where the hell it was all going anyway and why she was doing this crap in the first place. Carlson made a mental note to take her somewhere else in a few minutes. Like the master bedroom. No matter who or what they were, everybody reacted strongly and many times adversely to cocaine, and Carlson was a pro when it came time to gauge that reaction and use it somehow to get what he wanted. Most people changed completely when on coke, Carlson had noticed. Like Jekyll and Hyde. There were very few exceptions. Whatever was inside that person came roaring to the surface, exposed for all the world to see and judge. If you were basically an honest, happy secure type, you became the life of the party. Those types were few and far between and there were even dark demons lurking inside those individuals, which would come screaming to the surface soon enough. Usually, Carlson saw the dark side come out in people almost right away because there was something basically wrong with their character to begin with. Like if you were essentially a selfish, greedy, vicious individual, all those character defects were soon magnified a hundred times by cocaine and you would become something that no power on earth could deal with. All you wanted was more coke, and you would do anything to get more, no matter what it was or what it took to get it. Character defects. That was what it was all about, Carlson decided, cocaine the icing on the cake of the soul.

It was all a game, all an illusion. When the high is gone, you're left looking at something that scares the living hell out of you, left seeing something in the mirror that you would have never imagined existed in your worst nightmare. Take a couple of his own people, for example, Carlson thought. They liked to strip down to their underwear or get stark naked and just start fondling themselves right out in the open. It was sick and it was sickening. Carlson decided he wanted out and soon. Just take the money from this load and run like hell.

"Let me tell you something, Tommy boy," Carlson growled, looking Overton dead in the eye. "I learned some things about people long time ago. One of them is this. Since man first crawled his scroungy ass out of the cave, he's been looking for ways to get intoxicated and he's going to do it no matter what you do to try and stop it. We all got our own little games and head games we're into. Jake—gambling. You—that shit. Me—money and good-looking bitches. A couple of these others—fast cars and flashy clothes, and, yeah, you can see the sleazy exhibitionist assholes even among our ranks right here. We're the flip side of the creeps we bust, only there's a real thin line separating both sides. We're all the same underneath, it's what we do with that sameness that counts."

"Yeah, I know, I've heard the argument before. Can't beat 'em, join 'em."

"Something like that, only it's not that simple. At the turn of the century this shit was legal in this country and people could go into little street-corner parlors and do as much as they could take. Then they outlawed it, just like they did booze during Prohibition, but does the law ever stop people from wanting to take themselves away from themselves? Look at you. Why do you do it?"